HAUNTERS
AND
HAUNTINGS

MOTE
IDA MAE
MAY 12
DEC 2

HAUNTER'S TALE

HAUNTERS
AND
HAUNTINGS

Curated by J. Michael Roddy

Featuring tales from:

Dianna Bennett	Michael Gavin	Jeff Preston	Kevin Alvey	Randy Bates
Gene & Jim Schopf	Kyle LaFlamboy	Scott Tater Lynd	Ricky Brigante
Dave Cobb	Jessica Dwyer	Eddie McLaurin	Mike Schwalm	Ed Terebus
Matthew Sanderson	Christian Stokes

Accomplishing
Innovation Press

Published By: Accomplishing Innovation Press an imprint of 4 Horsemen Publications, Inc.

Accomplishing Innovation Press
℅ 4 Horsemen Publications, Inc.
PO Box 419
Sylva, NC 28779
4horsemenpublications.com
info@4horsemenpublications.com

Typesetting by Valerie Willis

Library of Congress Control Number: 2024938005

Paperback ISBN-13: 979-8-8232-0378-4
Hardcover ISBN-13: 979-8-8232-0392-0
Ebook ISBN-13: 979-8-8232-0391-3
Audiobook ISBN-13: 979-8-8232-0550-4

TABLE OF CONTENTS

FOREWORD IX

WHAT IS A HAUNTER? XIII

DIANNA BENNETT **1**
   Interview 2
   Bitten By a Spirit 5

MICHAEL GAVIN **9**
   Interview 10
   The Gaslight Apartments Ghost, Or My First Fright 15

JEFF PRESTON **19**
   Interview 20
   A Tale of Two Haunts 24

KEVIN ALVEY **31**
   Interview 32
   The Chronicles of Mr. Gore 35

RANDY BATES **45**
   Interview 48
   Bates Motel & Haunted Hayride 51

FIELD OF SCREAMS: GENE & JIM SCHOPF **69**
   Interview 74
   A Spotlight on One of America's Premier Haunted Attractions 81

KYLE LAFLAMBOY **107**
   Interview 109
   From Soccer Practice to Psych Ward 113

SCOTT TATER LYND **121**
   Interview 122
   Humor Collides with Horror 125

RICKY BRIGANTE **129**
   Interview 130
   #NOFILTER 134

DAVE COBB **139**
    INTERVIEW 140
    TANGIBLE MAGIC: MY HALLOWEEN WITH RAY BRADBURY 145

JESSICA DWYER **149**
    INTERVIEW 150
    THE TRIBES OF THE MOON 153

EDDIE MCLAURIN **159**
    INTERVIEW 160
    HISTORY OF THE WOODS OF TERROR 165

MIKE SCHWALM **169**
    INTERVIEW 170
    LOST WORLD 173

ED TEREBUS **179**
    INTERVIEW 180
    THE HAUNTED HISTORY OF EREBUS 185

MATTHEW SANDERSON **193**
    INTERVIEW 194
    ONE SUMMER NIGHT IN CHEROKEE 198

CHRISTIAN STOKES **205**
    INTERVIEW 207
    THE HAUNTED HAUNTED HOUSE 210

J. MICHAEL RODDY **217**
    INTERVIEW 218
    A HAUNTING IN A HAUNT 225

IMAGE CREDITS **239**

FOREWORD

O kay, what the hell do I know about haunted attractions? Well, I've built or supervised them all over the East Coast of this country. Sometimes they just pay to use my name. Some were lovely and scary, and one in particular—Tom Savini's Terrormania—was the best one I've ever seen.

There is a science to scaring people. Anyone can jump up and yell "boo" with a mask on, and that scare lasts about two seconds … maybe. And that's what I see in big, haunted attractions everywhere. It's just people jumping up and screaming at you. The best scares come from suspense. Show a monster, or a psycho, or a tentacle creature right off the bat and have it disappear into the house and now the scare has begun. We don't know when that thing is going to come out and get us.

When someone enters a haunted attraction, they are looking for what they think is going to startle them 'cause they don't want to be scared. Well, we know this, so they might enter what seemed like a padded cell with a body in a bed. We made the body move with a motor in the ceiling and invisible black fishline. So when you came in, you were like, "Oh yeah … that body … that body is going to do something." So you moved away from the bed to the outer part of the room … AND THEN THE WALL GRABBED YOU. Well, you know, *someone* behind the wall, but we misdirected you into their grasp. See, it doesn't have to be someone jumping up and screaming at you.

But you have to be careful. You cannot scare a group, and usually, they come through the house in a group of say eight, from the front. They won't budge from where they are if you do. You want to keep the group moving, so you scare them just behind the middle. That propels them forward. And you shouldn't have an exhibit that is like a three-act play where the group has to stand there and watch it unfold. It should continuously be happening.

At Terrormania, we gave the group a ten-foot length of rope, made up a ghost story, and said we couldn't guarantee their safety if they didn't hang onto the rope. This kept them together because sometimes they like to wander on their own, and it ensured their feet would step on the pad that activated the animatronics.

A haunted attraction should also be slightly annoying, and psychologically disturbing. It should bug you … literally. One I remember vividly had me traversing a long, dark hallway. Along the walls were the projected images of black bugs. Combined with the sound of crawling and scraping were Styrofoam peanuts spread all over the floor, so you felt like you were stepping on insects. Fishing line hung from the ceiling completed the illusion, so there was always something touching your face, and it made you feel like you were walking through spiderwebs. It doesn't always have to be people jumping up and yelling, "Boo." I'll keep repeating that.

It was disturbing to people who walked down a very dark and long hallway into a room—all of which was painted with small red and green and blue dots—where black lights made the glowing dots seem to fly off the walls in a 3-D effect. They were not ready for the agile guy wearing a black head-to-toe leotard, also painted with the same glowing dots, when he moved out of a corner and slid or crawled along one of the walls. Loud screams erupted from the psychologically disturbed patrons. See, it doesn't have to be someone jumping up and yelling, "Boo." I'll say it over and over again.

We had 27 rooms at Terrormania, and film companies were coming there to shoot 'cause we had a swamp, a cemetery, a subway, caves, a funeral parlor, and a lot of people never made it past the third room. The Spider Room. Use your imagination. We had "Pants Pissers." Mostly pregnant women.

One grand illusion I remember from Morris Costumes Haunted Attraction in Charlotte, North Carolina was entering an elegant Victorian set beautifully decorated with antique furniture and a massive mirror over an ornate fireplace. You walked into this room wondering what was going to happen. Is someone going to jump up and yell "Boo?" No, but what did happen is a ragged chiffon, blowing in the wind, white-costumed hideous ghost catapulted at you right THROUGH THE MIRROR! It was merely a beautifully framed hole in the wall above the fireplace, and everything on the other side matched the room you were in. You know … what a mirror would do. It was disconcerting and scared me genuinely.

Another one that stands out in my memory is one that Michael Roddy had a hand in creating at Universal for their annual Halloween Horror Nights when he worked there. It was traversing a massive hole in the floor many, I mean many, stories down below your feet. It gave me weak knees, and it was merely an enormous mirror on the floor reflecting the many levels above it. And then there was the floor of glass you walked over that was many stories below your feet. Again, shaky, queasy knees.

We love this stuff. We pay people to scare us. Like a service we seek. We do it at amusement parks, haunted attractions, and at the movie theatres where, yes again, we pay to be scared. We love to be scared, and we will go back as long as there are artists and thinkers out there willing to do it to us.

Pleasant dreams,

Tom Savini

WHAT IS A HAUNTER?

James-Michael Roddy

What is a Haunter? The term has come to prevalence in the last few years. When I was designing haunted experiences, we called them Haunted Houses. Then the terminology transitioned into Haunted Mazes with the idea that you could potentially get lost within the darkened spaces. The maze was quite the misnomer though, as it always seemed to be a contradiction to the operations that wanted the maximum throughput, hence why in many cases you have guides with flashlights showing you the way to the next room. But, like all things, once awareness of a trend sets in and it becomes part of a culture, we name it. Like Trekkies and Deadheads, the Designers/Operators of a Haunt are called Haunters.

The industry has certainly grown in the 25 years that I have been involved, and the benefit is that creativity allows for some genuinely terrifying experiences.

My first experience with a haunted house was when I was a child of probably six. I loved horror and was excited to visit a scary house … until I actually got in line. The more I looked at the structure, which in my nostalgic recollection looked exactly like the *Old Dark House*, the more anxious I became. The screams coming from the inside seemed to echo in the night. I chickened out. Years later, I was part of a haunted woods scenario with future Director Erik Hollander. He spent a full month building real structures along a wooded path. His attention to detail and story were only surpassed by his dedication.

Then when I moved to Orlando, I met David Clevinger, who brought me on board for Terror on Church Street. This was my first real experience with the business of haunted houses. What a phenomenal experience. I owe a lot to that old, haunted Woolworth building on Church Street (yes, it was really haunted). I was able to really see how David combined quality theatrics and genuine scares and even given the opportunity to help create.

Then I was cast as Norman Bates for a Halloween event at Universal Studios Florida. What a blast. I met Leonard and Jeanne Pickel, who designed the Psycho Path maze, and to this day they both call me Norman. Long story short, I turned that experience into a future career as a Halloween designer. I was involved in the creation of Halloween Horror Nights shows and experiences from 1995 until 2002 and then again from 2006 until 2009.

I love a good haunted house. I love the anticipation and the clues to what's to come. Within these pages are some of my friends who have been a part of the Haunt industry over the years. Our connections vary, but there is one particular, consistent thread; we love to scare. The promise of a scream is our fuel. We have all done it. Remember back through your life, and at some point, somewhere, you jumped out from a hidden space and yelled "Boo." That really is the core. We are all still saying "Boo," but now we do it much more elaborately. We also have a real love for the genre. We are fans of the things that go bump in the night. We are most closely associated with the films, as most of what we accomplish is a living horror film. We fabricate the story, we prepare the scenes, we rehearse the actors. The difference is a mix of traditional, living theatre where we can hear our audience react. We want them to feel every moment that we have been tirelessly creating, weeks, sometimes months in advance.

I am a Haunter. I love the experience of creating something in the hopes that it will give you nightmares, or at the very least, a sense of foreboding and dread.

So this book of tales is an opportunity to let our creativity loose on you in a new way. Inside are stories, drawings, photos, and a few true encounters that hopefully allow you inside. I hope to make this a yearly anthology, celebrating kindred spirits and allowing them to roam. Regardless, I hope you like what we have prepared.

DIANNA BENNETT

ianna Bennett and her alter ego, Luna Mystique, have been in the haunt industry for nearly two decades. She first stepped into haunting as therapy after losing her father in 1999. She worked at Busch Gardens' Howl-O-Scream from 2000 to 2014, bringing many memorable characters to life. Her favorite Howl-O-Scream personas include Mistress Macabre (the bewitching Dominatrix of Darkheart's Fear Fair), GiGi (one of the Killer Klowns), and Researcher Gama of the Experiment (who made sure you knew just what level of trouble you were about to get your hands into). She left Howl-O-Scream to follow her mentor, Scott Swenson, in a new, unique, hands-on, fully immersive, theatrical haunt experience as Maria Saavedra the Seductress, a 1920's era dominatrix. She was a favorite character each year. During the off season, she attends several Haunter conventions to keep on the cutting edge of the industry. She is a writer, actress, and massage therapist.

WHAT DO YOU LOVE ABOUT THE GENRE OF HORROR?

Horror can mean so many different things. It's not just blood, guts and gore. It can mean Dentist trips, ants, and spiders too. It's all about what scares you individually.

WHAT IS SOME OF YOUR FAVORITE HORROR LITERATURE?

I love the classics; Edgar Allan Poe, Shelley, and Stoker, but I'm a HUGE fan of writers like Dean Koontz, Clive Barker, Anne Rice, and Ray Bradbury. My favorite book when I was younger was *Nathaniel* by Dean Koontz

WHAT ARE SOME OF YOUR INFLUENCES?

Real life experiences, people I know, and places I've visited. I love historical events and what has transpired in the past. I like to weave and create them into a tapestry.

WHAT IS YOUR FAVORITE HALLOWEEN TREAT?

It's NOT candy corn. I have to say that it's probably triple chocolate Kit Kats. They don't come out frequently and they're incredibly delicious. Baring finding those, I really do enjoy Pumpkin Cheesecake, which only begins to come out around Halloween.

YOU ARE HOSTING THE PERFECT HALLOWEEN MOVIE MARATHON. WHAT ARE THE FILMS YOU CHOOSE AND WHY?

Hard Question. I wouldn't because I don't host, but I suppose, if I have to, it's going to start with something fun and light, like *Hocus Pocus* to set the mood, and really, who doesn't LOVE that movie? After that, we'd venture into a darker path, but I'd really have to think about it.

IF YOU COULD CONTINUE ANY HORROR STORY, WHAT WOULD IT BE?

I honestly don't know.

AS A DESIGNER OF HORROR THEATRE OR EXPERIENCES, EXPLAIN YOUR PROCESS.

I'm an actor in horror theatre, my process is simple; I give it my all. My characters are written within parameters, and I am allowed to bring them to life. I'm glad those who I work with trust me to do this.

WHEN IS THE LAST TIME YOU WERE GENUINELY SCARED BY SOMETHING SOMEONE CREATED?

Probably the first time I saw *Nightmare on Elm Street*. Or Even *Poltergeist 2*, the vomiting worm scene.

TELL US ABOUT YOUR CONTRIBUTION TO OUR BOOK. WHAT WAS THE INSPIRATION?

My contribution was a real-life experience. Something that actually happened when I worked at an event.

DESCRIBE THE PERFECT HALLOWEEN.

Cool air, dark skies, crisp autumn wind that swirls multi-colored leaves into tiny tornadoes at my feet. Somewhere in the Northeast, like Philly, so I can experience the change of the seasons and enjoy the plethora of Haunts that are up there. Good hayrides, Gothic mansions open for tours, ghost hunts, and seances. Anything to get a rise out of the senses.

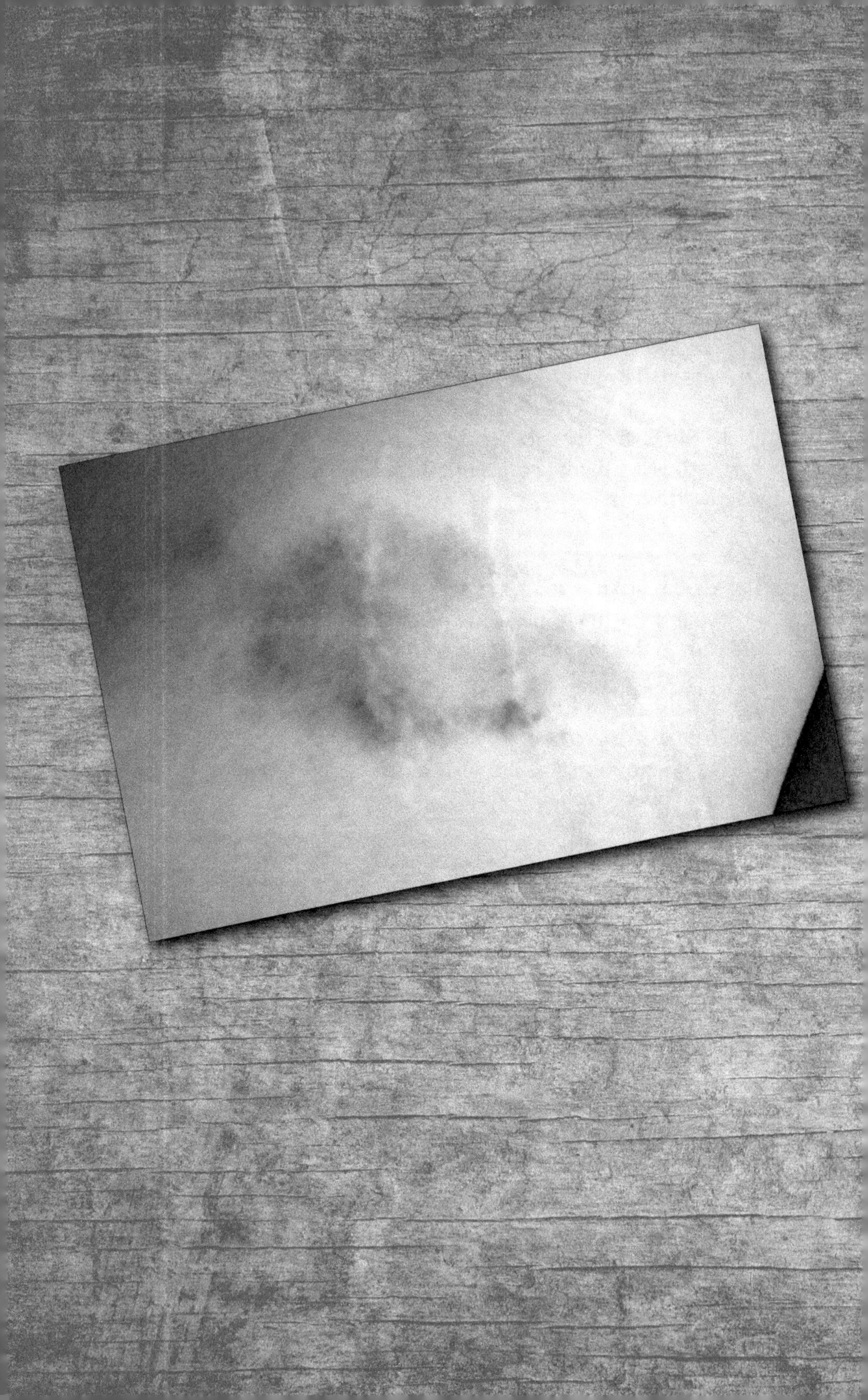

BITTEN BY A SPIRIT

I find it's far easier to write from experience rather than to have to craft something from the aether. So this should come as no surprise when I tell you this is a true story. It happened to me when I was working in Downtown Tampa at an upscale event called The Vault of Souls.

We weren't a "Haunt" as most people know them. There was no blood, no gore. No one in an absurd costume would jump out from the darkened recesses and shout "BOO!" at you. No, we were an immersive, theatrical experience. One you were invited to participate in; how deep you got was up to your own level of involvement. It was a unique and exciting venue for the market, something that not everyone "got."

The building that our event was held in was the original First National Bank of Tampa, where we occupied three floors. The Main floor had you at an elegant soiree with dancers and other entertainment, the upper floor, which is where our Tarot readers and aerialist performed to our guests' amazement, and then there was the basement, where the Vault actually was. This place was unique and where the story actually happens.

You see, this is a rare thing in Florida, a basement, but it's also the FIRST drive through for banking in the city of Tampa, among other things, and it's rumored to be haunted. I can honestly say, it's not a rumor but the truth. When they were preparing the building for our arrival, part of the floor in one area suddenly just "erupted," causing the folks working in that particular area to leave and not come back to work. If I remember my numbers correctly, it's over

35 people who started working on the build and that never came back after being disturbed.

We had many of the usual things happen, and by usual, I mean we heard our names called, phantom footsteps, and music boxes that would go off on their own, this stuff was creepy, but somewhat explainable. What was NOT explainable was the night I got bitten.

The night I got bitten, it was our second weekend into the run, and I believe a full moon. Our Tarot readers and psychics were all amped for the weekend, and one of them went downstairs to do a cleansing since we'd recently found out the name of a prospective spiritual resident. My room seemed to be an area of draw, whether that's due to me or to the building's design is neither here nor there, but Camile was drawn to my room and started her prayers. When she came up, I noticed that the moonstone at her throat was unusually cloudy and suggested she put it in salt and under the moonlight to clean it, and that's when she told me what she'd been up to. She'd gone through my specific area and done a cleansing, and the spirit (spirits?) there didn't want to go. She warned me I might be in for a little tumult that evening. She couldn't have been more right.

That evening, our guests were cantankerous, we had a few that needed to speak to security and the feeling in my room was decidedly off. My character was that of a 1920's dominatrix, and in as much, I was wearing a fully steel-boned corset, garters, the whole shebang. At one point in the evening, I felt something on my side. A touch? A pinch? I'm not sure, but it was beneath the corset, and it was itchy. During the course of the night I could try to scratch it through the fabric of the corset, but I couldn't actually scratch my skin.

During the evening's run, when no one was around, I heard someone call my name, and then felt someone touch my hair. The name thing, I thought was castmates calling for me, so I asked, and they were just waiting for the next round of guests. The touching of my hair? Nope, couldn't explain it. It was just strange.

After the show ended around 1:30 am and we went up to our dressing room to change back into our day wear, I felt great relief getting undressed; eight hours in a corset is not bad, but it felt good to be ME again. It was then that one of the other girls asked me,

"What happened?" I looked at my side in the mirror and there was what looked like a large bite mark on my side where the odd sensation had been that evening. It was sizeable, darker at the bottom than at the top, angry looking mark on my skin.

My guess is that the work our psychic did in my room riled the spirits up and they took it out on me. That's the first time I was ever "bitten" by a spirit.

MICHAEL GAVIN

As a fan of fear for over 40 years, writing for an entertainment news site and creating fantasy/horror themed photography currently fuels my passion for fright-filled fiendish fun.

With the help of a few friends, I created and conducted Orlando's very first haunted history tour: Orlando Hauntings (2000); a book detailing those spooky stories and first-hand experiences is in the works. Haunts and attractions like Terror on Church Street, Skull Kingdom, and Disney's Tower of Terror have been called "home" at one time or another. Photography and writing projects have appeared in *Playboy, Forbes, GHOST! Magazine, Orlando Weekly,* the City of Orlando website, *Gores Truly,* and *Inside the Magic.* Images have been used to promote fan conventions, Pirates Dinner Adventure and The Shallow Grave haunted attractions.

AS A DESIGNER OF HORROR THEATRE OR EXPERIENCES, EXPLAIN YOUR PROCESS.

Each image should tell a story. For each planned set, I try to work with the model to bring them into the creative process. Sometimes this involves transforming concepts they envision to life; others it's a collaborative effort which includes introducing elements of the shoot that he or she are fond of. In so doing, their investment in the creative process produces better images. For cemetery (and other dark themed photographs without models), usually the environment does most of the storytelling work.

WHEN IS THE LAST TIME YOU WERE GENUINELY SCARED BY SOMETHING SOMEONE CREATED?

Honestly, I cannot recall the last time I was scared beyond being startled by a jump scare at a haunted attraction. Instead, my reactions tend to lean towards admiration and inspiration.

TELL US ABOUT YOUR CONTRIBUTION TO OUR BOOK. WHAT WAS THE INSPIRATION?

I've enjoyed horror ever since discovering I could be the one controlling or contributing to the scare. This magical transformation occurred at the age of nine, after discovering a monster makeup book at the school book fair. Photography captured my interest in high school. With the advent of quality digital photography equipment, it was only natural that the two interests merged into a passion for creating creepy, cool pictures.

WHAT DO YOU LOVE ABOUT THE GENRE OF HORROR?

I really enjoy the ambiance and beauty of the genre. Dark, brooding, and mysterious elements (especially the music) provide great places to escape, meditate, and create.

WHAT IS SOME OF YOUR FAVORITE HORROR LITERATURE? FAVORITE AUTHOR?

I cannot pinpoint one favorite author, though lately Owl Goingback's work has been providing fiendishly fun nightmares. Overall, a good ghost story and/or diving into the history and backstories of Halloween and classic horror movies provides a delightfully dark escape.

WHAT ARE SOME OF YOUR INFLUENCES?

In addition to the monster makeup book that lured me into the genre, the work of Joshua Hoffine (check out his horror photography coffee table book!); creative creations of Christine McConnell; and cemetery photography of Sid Graves grant me inspiration. As making macabre miniatures (spooky dollhouses and similar) will provide my camera with fresh new material, Heather Tracy and Bentley House minis (check their Addams Family dollhouse) offer YouTube inspiration and instruction. But most of all, my mom influenced my journey into this tiny realm of terror as she used to make all kinds of miniature creations. Inheriting her tools didn't hurt either.

WHAT IS YOUR FAVORITE HALLOWEEN TREAT?

A well-decorated, spooky, sugar cookie. Crisp, not overly sweet, and fresh baked will tempt my taste buds beyond any candy.

YOU ARE HOSTING THE PERFECT HALLOWEEN MOVIE MARATHON. WHAT ARE THE FILMS YOU CHOOSE AND WHY?

Almost always, Classic horror (and/or a few well-done spin offs of these pioneering pictures) will take center stage. Never have been a fan of the hack/slay, overly gory modern movies. In my opinion, these classics offer sinister stories, great ambiance and offer subtle fear not found with most of today's films.

IF YOU COULD CONTINUE ANY HORROR STORY (BOOK OR FILM), WHAT WOULD IT BE?

Showtime's *Penny Dreadful* series ended too abruptly and left so much potential (both for the existing characters and new monsters) behind. Sorry, while the *City of Angels* spinoff was great period-centric entertainment, this was not the *Penny Dreadful* with monsters and spooky fun I was hoping for.

DESCRIBE THE PERFECT HALLOWEEN.

There's a slight chill cooling the nighttime air. A full moon accents the evening. Trick-or-treaters traverse the neighborhood, on a quest for sweet treasures. Eerie music offers ambiance for the monstrous sounds emanating from between foam tombstones and low-lying fog of what was once the front yard. Hints of hideous creatures lurk within the shadows. Headlights from what appears to be a haunted hearse illuminate the driveway. Within the garage-transformed laboratory, an eccentric mad scientist, vaguely resembling me, awaits his next victims, ready to reward their bravery with a handful of brightly wrapped confections... After this adventure fades away and the young would-be monsters have completed their adventure, this "mad scientist" retreats to the backyard bonfire to exchange ghost stories with friends and fiends. This magic meanders well into the enchanted evening.

BABY
LAND
3

13

THE GASLIGHT APARTMENTS GHOST, OR MY FIRST FRIGHT

For the longest time (even during research for the downtown ghost tours), I was a skeptic of most things that go bump in the night. I used to believe that, at least for most of the alleged hauntings I'd heard about, there was a logical and natural explanation to what was transpiring. The following account relates how one incident changed my mind and opened my eyes to the possibility of things unseen or unexplained. I have changed the names of those involved to protect their privacy. The Gaslight Apartments no longer exist; they have been renamed since this event took place…

I am not exactly sure when I met Lori; I think it was some time in 1996. Our first date took place one summertime Saturday afternoon and involved a casual lunch and light conversation. I was charmed with the opportunity to meet her then two-year-old daughter.

I seem to recall being intrigued yet skeptical when Lori first mentioned that the apartment she lived in was haunted. I was certain that there was a logical explanation for the apparent self-opening closet door in her daughter's room (perhaps the daughter opening the door in an attempt to get attention?) Soon arrangements were made for me to be there for an evening to witness the events firsthand (or, as I expected, gallantly dispel them). After dinner, the baby was put to bed, and I made a point to inspect the suspect door to ensure it was secured and wouldn't budge unless the door handle was deliberately and completely turned. Lori arranged the covers over her daughter in such a manner that we would be able to tell if the child was the one getting out of bed and opening that closet door.

Anxiety and duty evoked the urge to check on the room about two hours later. To my shock and horror, the closet door directly in front of the bed was clearly, and very much fully, open! Lori had been with me the entire time and her daughter's bedsheets were completely undisturbed. Timidly, we secured the suspect closet door again, and exited the room somewhat shaken and wondering if it would happen again.

We didn't have long to wonder—(note: this is about the time in a movie, where ominous music would begin to play).

Later, upon revisiting the dark room, a sense of eerie déjà vu crept in as we were again greeted to a once-secured closet door completely ajar and a peacefully sleeping little two-year-old girl, covers undisturbed. At this point Lori wanted to block the door, but caution prevailed (I didn't want anything to go flying into the child's bed). Instead, the baby was relocated to the couch and out of that room for the rest of the night. This game of opening and shutting the closet door continued throughout the evening, until we finally gave up around 2:00 am.

At one point, I recall noticing that a toy, which was resting against the far wall, had somehow made its way to the center of the room. All throughout the unnerving events, I recall experiencing a strong anxiety and kind of electricity in the air (a feeling I later came to know as the energy vibration that is associated with the presence of ghosts).

Finally, the sun began to break the night's darkness and it now felt "safe" to bravely venture into the small bedroom. What we discovered that morning astonished us beyond the previous evening's eerie activities. The closet with the mysteriously opening door had somehow shed all of its contents into a tangled heap on the closet floor. We found on a nightstand next to the bed, a coloring book, conspicuously opened to a page depicting a religious scene. It was the uncanny coincidence of the caption that caught our eye (and breath) "Jesus' friends were upset and suddenly he was there among them!" Was this a thinly veiled attempt at a message for the apartment's occupants? Even more bizarre was the earring that had managed to get stuck in the concrete ceiling as if it were a mere thumbtack upon a willing cork board.

Over time, the animated closet would prove to be the beginning of the challenge to my skepticism.

Lori kept pictures of her daughter in ascending stages of maturity neatly lined on one of the apartment walls. Upon returning home from an afternoon outing, we were shocked to find that all of the framed photos had somehow become tilted at an odd angle. However, the most mind-numbing event came to my attention shortly after receiving a frantic call from Lori just as I was leaving work. She implored me to come over to the apartment immediately. When I arrived, I was stunned by what greeted me in her daughter's room.

In the center of the carpet was an upturned stool. Stacked very much like a house of cards was every toy the child owned, very delicately balanced. The toy sculpture reached beyond my ability to touch the top (and Lori is quite a bit shorter than me). This shook me to the very core and was the tipping point to a more open point of view towards the paranormal.

Shortly after that scare, we shared our other-worldly accounts with a local psychic. We soon learned that we were dealing with the spirit of a young girl, quite possibly hiding in the closet of that bedroom. What could have frightened this child so badly? Was she trying to tell us something? After discussing the events and information we had just learned, Lori revealed that there had been a fire some years ago that had damaged the apartment complex. Allegedly the fire started in the very same apartment she called home.

Lori and I drifted apart shortly after these events, though not for any reasons related to the insane and alarming activity in that apartment. In fact, I do not know if the events even still occur. I am, however, now a definite believer in the paranormal.

JEFF PRESTON

Born in Ohio in 1958 and raised in Tennessee, Jeff Preston has had a lifetime fascination with monsters and all things 'spooky.' He has been a professional illustrator for over thirty-three years. Inducted into the prestigious New York Society of Illustrators in 2006, he also serves on the membership committee. Having enjoyed a prolific career in publishing and advertising, his monster art is what he is best known and awarded for. His art has appeared on the covers of *Famous Monsters of Filmland*, *Little Shoppe of Horrors*, *Monsterscene*, and *Monsterpalooza*. From home haunt to the professional attraction "Terror on the Square" in Gallatin then Nashville Tennessee (2000 – 2002), his approach was the same as in art. Highly-detailed, dramatic lighting, and atmosphere are all trademarks of his creative endeavors. His home studio is based just outside of Nashville, and he is always open for work.

YOU ARE HOSTING THE PERFECT HALLOWEEN MOVIE MARATHON. WHAT ARE THE FILMS YOU CHOOSE AND WHY?

1. *Frankenstein VS the Wolfman…* the opening scene in the cemetery holds a vivid memory. It would set the tone for a creepy night ahead.

2. *Dracula has Risen from the Grave…* classic Hammer, great visuals that even today rank high on the shudder scale. Dracula pulling the stake out, the priest dumping the female corpse out of the new, dug up coffin… still sends shudders up and down my spine!

3. 1979 *Dracula* with Frank Langella for one scene alone it makes the cut. Mina in the mines… for me the creepiest scene of all time!

4. *The Exorcist…* reasons not needed; the uneasy horror of this film stays with you YEARS after seeing it for the first time. I'm still apprehensive about watching it … but I'm hosting the marathon and out to scare my guests! ;)

5. *The Omen…* Classic horror that cannot be excluded.

6. *Trick R Treat…* this film to Halloween is what *A Christmas Story* is to Christmas. It has to be included.

7. Finally, *Halloween…* after remakes and countless sequels, going back we can really appreciate the genius of John Carpenter in making this film, it fires on all cylinders and is a perfect finale for the marathon.

IF YOU COULD CONTINUE ANY HORROR STORY, WHAT WOULD IT BE?

The really good ones need no continuance, they stand alone. That's why sequels rarely work or rise to the level of the original. The only exception would be *The Bride of Frankenstein.*

2011's *Don't be afraid of the Dark* I would like to see continued because the teeth-coveting Homunculi are such cool little creatures.

AS A DESIGNER OF HORROR THEATRE OR EXPERIENCES, EXPLAIN YOUR PROCESS.

Home Haunting, the goal was to set a mood and just scare people with various scenes. As a professional, I tried to design the attraction around a storyline. That made for a flow and purpose to the haunt. How many took the time to actually read the story, I haven't a clue, but from a creative standpoint, it gave structure to the attraction.

WHEN IS THE LAST TIME YOU WERE GENUINELY SCARED BY SOMETHING SOMEONE CREATED?

Never, I'm a haunter's worse audience for a scare. I'm more taken by the creation I'm seeing, the scene, the detail, the costuming, and the makeup, to even remotely be startled.

TELL US ABOUT YOUR CONTRIBUTION TO OUR BOOK. WHAT WAS THE INSPIRATION?

The concept of gathering stories from Haunters, who are the most creative group of people I know, is a noble effort that I'm honored to contribute to. Haunting is a true art form and shining the spotlight on its creators will hopefully bring a whole new appreciation of the creativity and ingenuity that goes into it.

DESCRIBE THE PERFECT HALLOWEEN.

Going back to the roots of home haunting is a dream I have. An elaborate, yet simple yard haunt that trick-or-treaters have to navigate to get their candy. It creates golden memories that are never forgotten.

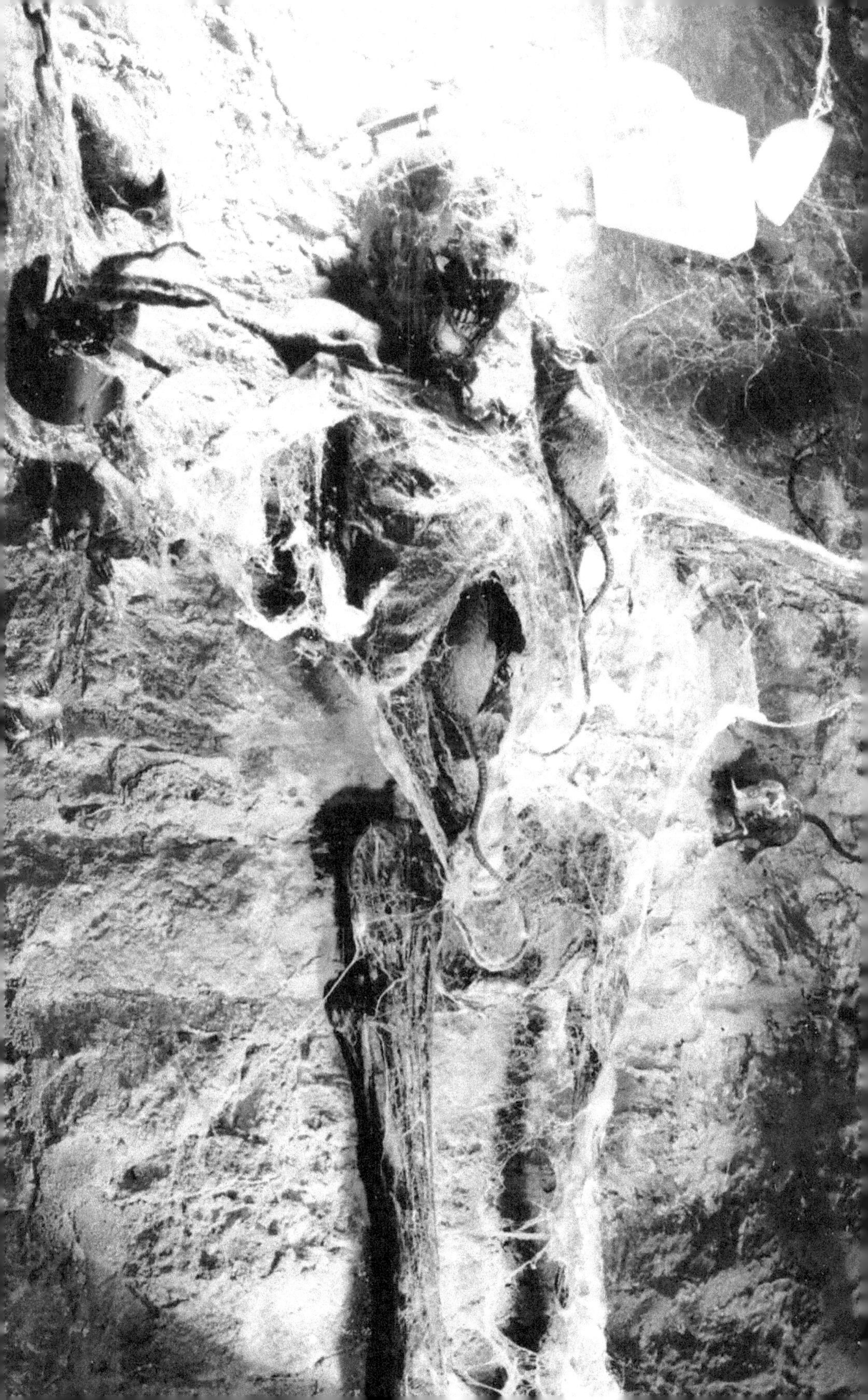

A TALE OF TWO HAUNTS

In 1973, the Jaycee's Haunted House opened their first haunted house in my hometown of Gallatin, Tennessee, it was somewhat of a nationwide trend at the time. I was 14 and jumped at the chance to work in the haunted house. For a monster kid, this was a dream come true. I was placed in a coffin beside another coffin with a mannequin… mainly because nobody else would get in the coffin. One night, a lady with her son came in and leaned over the ropes saying, "I swear this one looks real." I then reached up out of the coffin, and she hit the wall behind her and fainted dead away… I was instantly hooked on the art of the scare!

A couple more years followed with me working with the Jaycees, who gradually utilized more of my creative input. From a kid in a coffin to designing rooms and the scares that went with them, I literally was like a kid in the candy store. Of course, then came high school, adulthood, and like most things of youth, it just kind of faded away.

In 1994, I attended the nation's foremost model kit show, Wonderfest, in Louisville, Kentucky. That year, as it was every year, Bob Burns was the number one honored guest. The banquet proved to be a milestone for me. Bob treated us to footage of his legendary Halloween shows in Burbank, California. Everything magical about Halloween was captured in that footage. The style and craftsmanship that went into the shows was remarkable. The sets, costuming, and makeup were of Hollywood quality, which they should have been. Most of Bob's friends who helped out were working special-effects professionals in Hollywood, including a young, future multiple Oscar winner for makeup, Rick Baker. The one thing that stood out was the fact that everyone involved was having a blast, especially Bob. The seed was planted. I went away from Louisville with one goal in mind, to create the Halloween magic I remembered as a youth.

That fall, I started by carving a few pumpkins (the Pumpkin Masters carving tools we're still relatively new to the market), decorated my front hallway, and dressed up as a welcoming, ghoulish host. I had the time of my life and thrilled the dozen or so trick-or-treaters that graced my door.

How could anybody be excited over 12 visitors? The fact of the matter is I lived on a dark, dead-end street and had never had any trick-or-treaters before, so for me this was a significant victory.

The following year, I enlisted the help of six friends. We blocked off most of the walkway leading to my front door. We had a fog machine, black lights and strobes, custom fangs, and a hidden microphone that altered my voice to a chilling demonic echo. We had over a hundred visitors; word was starting to spread.

1996 was a pivotal year. *Monsterscene*, a magazine I did illustrations for released a Bob Burns special at the end of the previous year. I illustrated the cover, enabling me to become involved with Bob on a one-to-one basis. It was a dream assignment, and the cover turned out to be my most significant work to date, not to mention my first monster magazine cover! More than anything, it opened a dialogue between Bob and myself, and by this time my skill as a pumpkin artist had grown. I was asked to do a demonstration on a Nashville-based noon talk show. I showed how to carve a Bob Burns face on the pumpkin and talked about my Halloween shows at the house. Attendance that year grew to over 300; we were now firmly entrenched as a Halloween tradition.

In 1997 we expanded our production to the backyard; this allowed me to use the new deck I had built that spring. We wove our way in and out under the floor and blocked off the entire back of my house, creating a terrifying journey of mazed horror! Our production value significantly increased. Again, I gave the pumpkin-carving demonstration on television, plugging the show in the process. Attendance exploded! We ran 700 screaming, terrified visitors through in two and a half hours, another hundred

were turned away after we shut down for the evening. I was starting to get the feeling I just might be onto something here, and I kept the same blueprint in 1998.

The same route was taken by visitors, but we redesigned our scenes and polished the show to an even higher level. I had a new friend that came on board that worked heavily in theatrical set design and lighting. His expertise, not to mention his lighting equipment, brought us to where I would've stacked the show against any local commercial attraction. Our exit polling confirmed this. The comment most commonly heard was "I went to all the haunted houses in Nashville, but this was the best! You guys scared the crap out of me to me!" That was a standing ovation. Our numbers declined that year, but the quality of visitors made up for the drop in attendance. From opening to closing, all we heard was constant screaming.

In 1999, I was indecisive. Having spent a great deal of money and sweat equity landscaping my home, I did not want to disturb my efforts. The passion just wasn't there. I had run out of ideas, and my desire to start production was entirely absent. Then I ordered the video series *Hauntworld: The Movie* a series spotlighting the various haunted attractions across the country, and the bug bit! Suddenly new ideas started popping up, and my creative juices overflowed. My crew, now 35 Haunters, came back for more. I had been consulting with Bob Burns every season, always asking how do you do this or that, he was always gracious sharing his knowledge and expertise. We expanded the show around the house and reversed the route, our exit the previous year became the entrance and vice versa. We started production earlier, reducing my Halloween season anxiety. I knew inside that I had taken the show as far as I could at the house, so this was the final year of the House on Haunted Hill. We fine-tuned, polished the show, and were about to present a Halloween night deserving of Bob's Seal of approval. The attendance that final year was off the charts. Emergency management directed traffic in front of my house and at the end of my street, where cars were lined up for almost half of a mile. Close to a thousand people in a little under 3 hours for a road that never had a trick-or-treater, this was amazing. Since that final year, there hasn't been another, as a matter of fact.

While posting my promotional flyers on the town square, I kept noticing the availability of building space. The little voice in my head spoke—this is where I need to move the show!

A building on the square that was actually haunted was secured, and plans began for 2000 and Terror on the Square. Now was the building that Terror on the Square located actually haunted?

The storylines that were written to design the attraction around were interwoven with actual local history. The Lackey Cave was real, although probably not as widespread as legend made it out to be, running underneath the entire town. Of course, I didn't care one way or the other. I just embellished the tale tenfold. That somehow got the attention of area ghost hunters. One day I got a call from a lady wanting to investigate. She told me she was a psychic. I explained that the story, The Mortuary of Madness, was totally fictional, but she still wanted to come and take a look. The day arrived, and there was a knock on the door. Just my luck, she reminded me of Tangina, the older psychic lady from *Poltergeist*. She did bring a friend with her and immediately told her when she stepped inside the building, "Oh it's upstairs."

Now let's backtrack a few weeks. One Friday night, I was doing a radio interview during halftime at the local football game broadcast. My right-hand man, Mark King, was busy working on the steps to the fake elevator we had built a few days before. I left him there to work while I slipped out to do the interview. When I came back in an hour or so, he was gone. I immediately called and said, "Where are you, get back up here, we've got to finish this tonight!" He said dead seriously, "Look I heard you on the radio, all the doors were locked, and I knew I was the only one here, but I heard someone walking directly above me, and I got the hell out!"

I laughed, called him a wuss, and to get back up there. He did, we continued to work without incident, but I could tell he was legitimately spooked.

Now back to the "Run to the light" lady. When we got upstairs, she walked a few steps in and grabbed the side of the left side of her head saying, "I have a pain here" and then proceeded to say the same thing about her right arm. I thought to myself "Oh brother what a load of cra…" Then it dawned on me, she was standing directly over where Mark had been working on the elevator steps and heard the footsteps. The hair immediately went up on the back of my neck.

Still skeptical, I took her along the rest of the square, and when we hit the upstairs entrance to a corner bank, she immediately grabbed her throat and said she couldn't breathe. What she couldn't have known was that this was where a bank president had hung himself years earlier, it wasn't publicized, and very few knew about it. She could be the real deal after all.

The next year I continued the storyline, incorporating the Civil War and Union General Eleazer A. Paine, who held my hometown under a siege that reminded me of Vlad the Impaler! Aha … Civil War vampires, I had my theme!

In my research, I found something interesting. After the war, there was a caretaker, a Confederate veteran of the war, that took care of the downtown buildings. He had lost his right arm and suffered a wound on the left side of his head during battle.

That year, as the one before, Mark wasn't the only one who heard someone walking upstairs, seemed everyone did but me. However, I was upstairs when the phone rang on a postseason evening, one of my workers went to answer it, then realized the phone wasn't even plugged in! We called it a night.

KEVIN ALVEY

Kevin, aka Mr. Gore, has been creating props for films, theme parks, and haunted attractions since he was 15 years old. With over 35 years in the Halloween and Haunt industry, Kevin is the Creative Director and owner of Gore Galore Inc.

AS A DESIGNER OF HORROR THEATRE OR EXPERIENCES, EXPLAIN YOUR PROCESS.

Well, being a haunted house vendor, I either develop products from my own desires or to fill the needs of a customer. If a client asks for something specific, then we will put together sketches for approval of the idea until the design is approved. Then we will sculpt, mold, cast the creation, and create an armature to perfectly fit that foam creation. Then we finally put these pieces together and then send them to paint. After the painting is completed, we assemble it together. If we need to create sound effects, then we find the perfect sounds. We test out those sounds, then install them on the controller for the creature. Our final step is to test the system, and finally crate up and ship it to the customer.

Now if I do something without an order first, then we do all the same steps just without a client financing it first.

WHEN IS THE LAST TIME YOU WERE GENUINELY SCARED BY SOMETHING SOMEONE CREATED?

My Son! My wife and I created him. And it is his daily game to try to scare me. And he gets me sometimes.

TELL US ABOUT YOUR CONTRIBUTION TO OUR BOOK. WHAT WAS THE INSPIRATION?

Just trying to answer these questions honestly and with a hint of humor.

WHAT DO YOU LOVE ABOUT THE GENRE OF HORROR?

Because it isn't mundane. I think horror allows people to deal with the fear of death on an easier level. Death is terrifying to most, and horror allows them to come closer to experiencing it without fear of harm.

WHAT IS SOME OF YOUR FAVORITE HORROR LITERATURE? FAVORITE AUTHOR?

Old school Monsters. Mary Shelly.

WHAT ARE SOME OF YOUR INFLUENCES?

This list is non-exhaustive since I try to learn from everything.

Jim Henson, *Dark Crystal, Labyrynth, Time Bandits, Giger,* on and on we go. I am a puppet creator, so this list helped inspire the creations I have built.

WHAT IS YOUR FAVORITE HALLOWEEN TREAT?

Dark Chocolate. Everything Dark Chocolate.

YOU ARE HOSTING THE PERFECT HALLOWEEN MOVIE MARATHON. WHAT ARE THE FILMS YOU CHOOSE AND WHY?

Black and white Universal Monsters films and the silent *Nosferatu.*

Because I think these are what set the stage in my life to become dedicated to Halloween, and what would help carry others into the Halloween world.

IF YOU COULD CONTINUE ANY HORROR STORY (BOOK OR FILM), WHAT WOULD IT BE?

The life of a haunter! LOL It is all I know!

DESCRIBE THE PERFECT HALLOWEEN.

We used to not always decorate since I live Halloween 24/7, but as soon as we had our son, I found myself headlong into building and decorating. So now it would be building ALL the props we have on display and having the yard full of creations my son and I built together. Tons of devious Scarecrows and lots of wooden, silhouetted characters, backlit with led rope lights. Then TONS of trick-or-treaters since we usually do not get many at all since we are in a small town.

THE CHRONICLES OF MR. GORE

Kevin R. Alvey AKA Mr. Gore is a person who is aware he was made by his experiences, and the following is a chronicle of some of those experiences. And some other ramblings mixed in for good measure.

When I was very young, my father left me, my mother, and two sisters to fend for ourselves. I still do not really know why but that really isn't important here. What is important is that my mother began to travel to wherever the next job arose. This led us to many places around Kentucky and Indiana, and then most importantly to Orlando, Florida. My mother went to work at Disney World in a mask and novelty shop. I spent quite a bit of time in that little mask shop just staring at all the bizarre masks and allowing my imagination to take me to other worlds. It was here at Disney I also discovered the Haunted Mansion. I was lucky enough to get to spend what felt like days riding through the attraction taking in all the detail around me from the elevator with the stretching por-traits to the hitchhiking ghosts and everything in between. I think I was most astounded by the hitchhiking ghost. I really thought I had made a friend who was coming home with me.

My mother took us on another journey that led us around again and somehow ended up in Evansville, Indiana for another job opportunity. When I was 10, my mother met my soon to be stepfather. They married soon after and moved all of us (my sisters Kellie and Frances and three stepbrothers Mike, Jeff, and David) to Newburgh, Indiana. I did not know yet, but Newburgh was to be a pivotal place and time in my life. Newburgh would be my home for many years, and also the place where several events would happen that began to shape me into what I am today, "A twisted freak with delusions of horror and gore."

On one such occasion, and several others to follow, I was to be the butt to many of my stepbrothers' jokes.

One moonlit night, all the boys took a walk in the woods to an abandoned house. We all went inside, roaming around and just taking in the atmosphere of the vacant, condemned structure. We all decided we should go into the basement to check it out. Well, all three stepbrothers turned and ran back up the steps and locked the door behind them, leaving me in the pitch black without a flashlight. It was absolute darkness. I could not see my hand in front of my face. My adrenaline was pumping. All of a sudden I felt something touch my shoulder, so I turned and came face to face with blood-red, glowing eyes. I turned again and ran as best I could up the stairs and began banging on the door until they let me out. The odd thing is that I still do not know if there was actually anything in that basement, or if it was just my overactive imagination.

My stepbrothers were simply trying to be cruel to the outsider, but what they didn't realize was they were feeding the beast that would soon arise and devour everything in its path. They awoke in me a morbid imagination, and a creative drive looking for an outlet. The adrenaline rush was like nothing I had ever had before, and I wanted more. In a few short years, I was to discover everything I had dreamed of.

At the age of fifteen, I was working at a local pizza shop making deliveries. One October evening, I looked across the street and noticed an eerie dark structure I had never really noticed before. The Newburgh Civitan Haunted House (www.newburghhauntedhouse.com) had opened and was attracting a huge crowd, and I was drawn to the excitement. The line was wrapping all the way down the street.

When my shift was over, I went over that evening and began asking questions about the event. I was lucky enough to come face to face with Dan Fischer, one of the organizers in charge of the haunted house. Dan was nice enough to give me a tour of the haunted attraction.

The building was three stories tall, with Werewolves crawling all over the attraction and a giant skull was mounted on the front of the building. When the entrance would open, the dry ice fog would roll down a flight of stairs and a werewolf, on his knees, would slide all the way down the stairs and out the door. As you entered, werewolves would pop up from under the fog and take off like bolts of lightning. When you reached the top of the stairs and made the first turn, there was a casket with a live vampire within it. Another scene had a Frankenstein monster chained to the wall. The strobes would start flashing and the Monster would begin to struggle and break the chains. Then the lights went out, and you just didn't know where the monster was. I also noticed a bridge with a bottomless pit illusion. They also used what they refer to as a "Double Whammy." It is a scene with two actors that can startle the customers from opposite sides at the same time. It makes the customers feel trapped. Another fun scene had a clown theme with a body mounted on the wall hanging upside down, decapitated. The head was placed on a birthday cake.

Also, there was a long, tilting hallway that started straight and ended turned at a 30-degree angle. The scene that made a real impression on me was a live, half victim mounted on the wall. It was an effective illusion and pretty easy to pull off. I was impressed by the attraction and extremely grateful for the kindness shown to me by Dan. He made such an impact on me that starting the next day I began working with the Newburgh Civitans, helping them with their Haunted house year after year.

It has been two decades, and all I can say is thank you for letting me be a part of your event.

Since joining the Civitan club, I have been involved in every aspect of the haunted house from design, layout, construction, fiscal issues, fire codes, actor training, and the key aspect, prop construction.

Some of the things I have done over the years for and with the haunted house has led to developing the skills to become an experienced artist in the FX and prop-making field. Some of the items I have done are:

A drop ceiling effect: to this date it still drops patrons to the floor every time. I built a frame out of 1x4 clear yellow pine, boxed up the ends like a tube, and mounted eyebolts and cable all the way through, the facing is 3/4 plywood and it is suspended from the ceiling with a block and tackle at either end. Young girls typically operate the effect. It shakes the entire house when it hits the wall.

Stick Boy: A 7' skeleton marionette which the base form was whittled out of 2x2s and given an alligator type head out of plywood, 12-gauge wire, and papier-mâché. The whole skeleton is fully articulated. You can make this thing fly around inside its cage grabbing through the bars from a raised platform. It is suspended from an oversized marionette control system, with the head operated independently with a separate control. You can turn the head side to side, up and down, or snap the jaws wildly and shake the head.

Illusion torso: I also took a torso Dan made several years before and animated the spine with cable and springs and then adding a drive motor. It was pretty gross seeing this spine slap around in KY jelly (It is safe for latex props since it is water based) for an illusion where it appears a victim has been cut in half with a circular saw.

Body Bowl or Ice Chest: (a name recently thought of by John Burton) I made an upper torso with severed arms and decapitated head, with a large gaping chest wound out of fiberglass to put a runny, bloody concoction an actor could appear to be eating out of. It was a pretty gross effect. I devised it for the "Wild Boy of Borneo" scene.

Vato-Lac2: I purchased an old, beat-up Chevy Nova and modified it for guerrilla marketing. We used to drive it in parades, cruise on weekends, and show up in some of the weirdest places with it. It demanded attention with bloody, sheet-metal teeth and a spring-loaded tongue that would flap in the wind. How could I not have a blast when I was doing things like this?

But two of the most important things I ever did with the Haunted House, I did not do alone. Enter Eric Ridenour, talented artist and soon to become lifelong friend.

Together we built two pieces that would become the backbone to how we would start our new business, Gore Galore.

Spooky Ernie: A 15' backpack rod puppet. He was sculpted out of bead board and constructed out of lumber and lots of fiberglass. We just thought, what could we do that would be a real challenge just to see if we could do it. We did it, and what an impression this bad boy makes. Ten years later he still scares the bejeezes out of customers.

Dizzy Lizzy: A dead, rotting ballerina standing over 9' tall doing a pirouette on a huge music box. Her head remains forward staring at the customers while her body spins wildly around in circles.

We have created many animations and props for The Newburgh Haunted House and all I can say is thank you. I was given the opportunity to learn, develop my skills, make wonderful friends, and find a direction. I found my destiny and for the first time in my life, I knew what I wanted to do with my life, and things were about to get even better.

When I was eighteen, something wonderful happened. I met Kathy Pepe. Simply stated, she and I were together for 20 years. I brought her to the haunted house, and she was hooked. She fell in love with it, and she became seriously involved. When the haunted house moved to their new location, she and I built a 16' tall x 20' wide clown-head façade. The customers entered the mouth on their way to the entrance. One day we were in a local novelty shop ,"Nick Nackery," and Larry, the owner, informed us of a Halloween tradeshow he thought we should attend, The Halloween Party Show in Chicago. So in 1997, we went as buyers for the Newburgh haunted house. I was like a kid in a candy store but at the same time overwhelmed by it. This day became another pivotal moment in my life. Because this was the moment that we decided we were going to start a haunted house prop production business. I was actually very unsure of my skills, after all, I had only made props for a local haunted house, even though I did have design, engineering, sculpting, molding, and finishing skills. However, Kathy was certain that we could get the job done.

When we returned, Kathy, Eric Ridenour (a good friend whom I built many monsters with), and myself got together for a brainstorming session. We talked about name after name but then Gore Galore literally fell out of my mouth and that was it. It was certain. It encapsulated everything we were going for. It grabbed your attention and sticks in your mind, and it has a morbid sense of humor. It tells you just what we do.

The products we come up with seem to come about the same way the name did, on a whim, by instinct. MY favorite items are ones that just came to mind and I immediately put them into action, like the Corpsification Kit, Botulism Buffet, Dip Head, Motor Head Animation, and Meat Head Mobile. The mobile was designed as a way to display the heads at Transworld with a minimum of required space, but it turned out to be a best-selling item. Gore Galore is about the joy and love of Halloween, and these items encompass that idea. I think that may be seen by others and can explain their popularity. I believe our enthusiasm and love of Halloween is what will lead us to create innovative and inspiring new products with great pride in our work. All I want to do is have fun creating the best quality products at the best possible price.

I think this may help explain why we have done business with some of the biggest names in the industry, from: Queen Mary, Multiple Six Flags locations, Busch Gardens, and Clear Channel, to hundreds of other haunted attractions per year. We have also been lucky enough to have some of our work used in several Indie films, and we are very proud to mention our work has been used by USA television in several of their productions. The main one to mention is *Law and Order Special Victims Unit*. We actually had three corpses (Chester, Lester, and Blubbo) used in the same episode "Wrath." And I have been told one of our corpses was used in an episode of *the Mole*.

One thing I find very amusing, we have had several pieces used in a few Shakespearean plays. One thing that is very exciting to me is seeing our work used in other attractions. It is just so fulfilling knowing that our work has an impact on others, despite the fact that the effect might have something to do with bodily fluids.

Gore Galore has given me a second childhood. I see things in a whole new way. I get inspiration from everything from films, toys, reading, to talking with friends. It all leads me somewhere. The only problem is that it tends to be the only thing I think about. I say, "I am very focused." Others say, "I have a one-track mind."

All I can say is that I have had many things happen in my life, and I regret nothing. Now here it is over 25 years later, and nothing has changed. It has all led me to where I am right now, and made me the person that I am, "A twisted freak with delusions of horror and gore."

Thanks for your time, and keep gore alive!

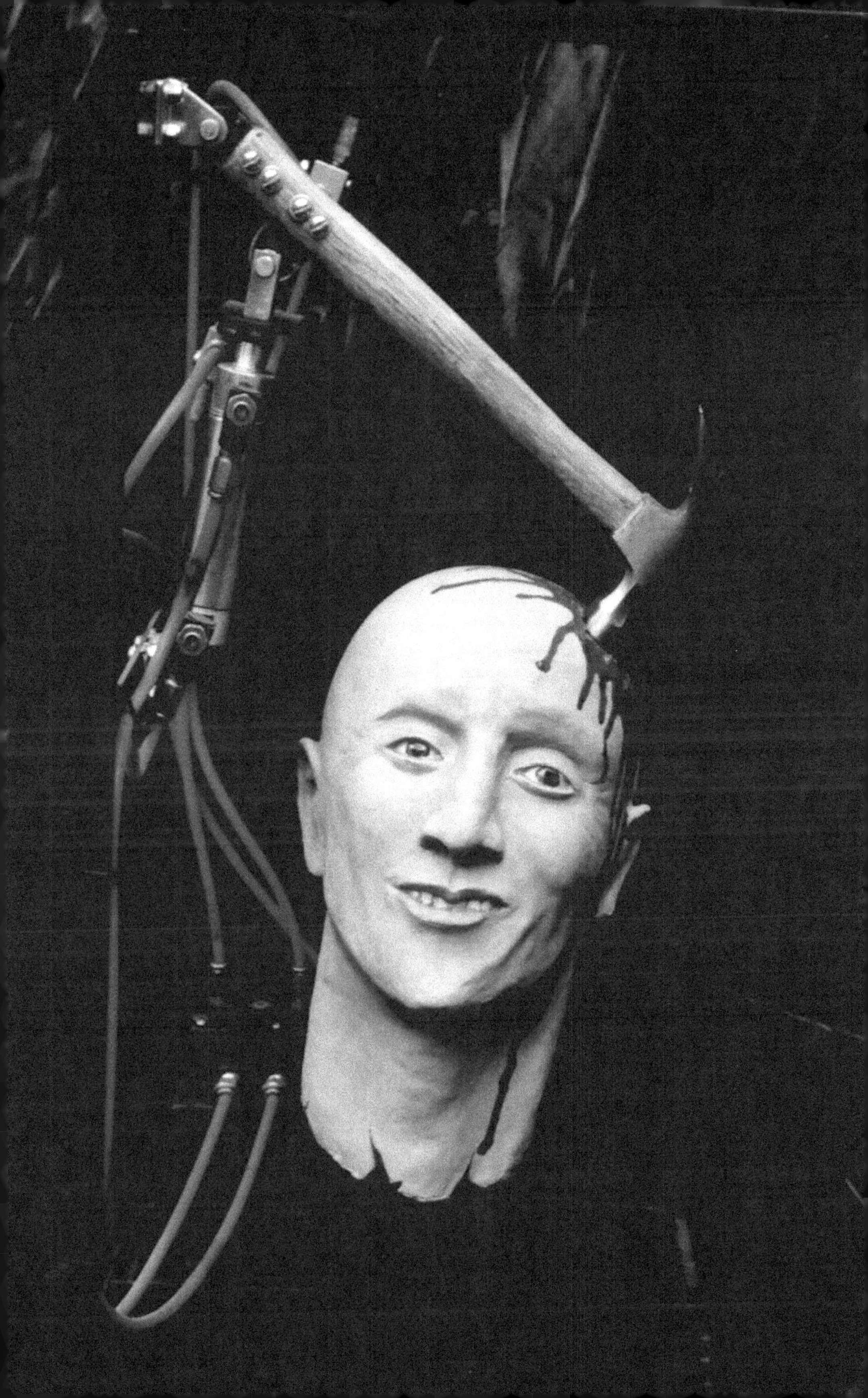

RANDY BATES

Randy Bates is the owner of Arasapha Farm located in the Philadelphia suburbs. He has a bachelor's degree from York college and has lived on the farm for most of his life. Randy has been a member of Edgmont Fire company 64 for 25 years and served as the captain of the fire police unit. He served on the township planning commission from 2005 to 2014 and served on the board of supervisors. He also currently serves as a board member on the Delaware County Conservation District and is a past board member of the PA Farm Bureau. Randy is a founding member of the Edgmont Business and Professional Association, and a founding member of IAHA, International Association of Haunted Attractions, Past board member, Founding member of the Haunted House Association and past president.

Randy has been an advocate for haunted attraction safety. He has taught seminars in Haunted House Code Compliance, Hayride attraction safety and outdoor events safety to the Pennsylvania State inspectors' course twice a year since 2007. In 2014 Randy was appointed to chair the ASTM International Hayride Safety Standard. Over the next five years, this standard was continually revised and finally adopted in 2020.

Randy and his wife, Anne, raised six children and currently have nineteen grandchildren, most of who live on or near the farm Beside the Haunted attractions, Randy and Anne run the Harvest Hayride, a children-themed fall activity, and Arasapha Tree Farm, growing and selling Christmas trees. Another business Randy has is the Bates Mobile Experience, run by Ben's wife Nicole. It consists of mobile escape room trailers, an axe throwing trailer, and mobile laser tag system.

WHEN IS THE LAST TIME YOU WERE GENUINELY SCARED BY SOMETHING SOMEONE CREATED?

I can't remember when I was scared by something like that.

TELL US ABOUT YOUR CONTRIBUTION TO OUR BOOK.

I wanted to write about the people who made our business successful. I know I'm leaving out a lot of folks, but this is the short version of a 33-year business.

WHAT DO YOU LOVE ABOUT THE GENRE OF HORROR?

I like suspense. I like unique movies and attractions.

WHAT IS SOME OF YOUR FAVORITE HORROR LITERATURE? FAVORITE AUTHOR?

Of course, Stephen King stands out. I also like Dean Koontz, especially the book *Watchers*.

WHAT ARE SOME OF YOUR INFLUENCES?

Friends and family. We try very hard to be unique, so you will never see Freddy or Jason running around our woods. About 20 years ago, Kane Hodding came out expecting VIP treatment. I gave him and his girlfriend passes, and when he was through the attractions he asked why we didn't have a Jason scene. I just told him we didn't use movie monsters.

WHAT IS YOUR FAVORITE HALLOWEEN TREAT?

Jack Daniels

YOU ARE HOSTING THE PERFECT HALLOWEEN MOVIE MARATHON. WHAT ARE THE FILMS YOU CHOSE, AND WHY?
Phantasm, Oculus, The Shining, Scream, The Exorcist, The Omen, House of Usher, Zombieland, Nosferatu, It, The Babadook, and of course, *Psycho.*

IF YOU COULD CONTINUE ANY HORROR STORY (BOOK OR FILM), WHAT WOULD IT BE?
The Stand, by Stephen King.

DESCRIBE THE PERFECT HALLOWEEN.
Ending a Haunt season with no injuries.

BATES MOTEL & HAUNTED HAYRIDE

For 32 years, Arasapha Farm has been putting on a Halloween Haunted Attraction. This is the story of the people that have made it successful over the years.

It all started because our neighbor stopped hosting a charity haunted trail on his farm. In 1990, he had over 5,000 people show up and they proceeded to destroy his forest, breaking props and throwing trash around. I saw the potential to make a few bucks and have fun at the same time, however, I wanted to be different. We were already operating hayrides to picnic areas and bonfires, had four tractors and hay wagons, and had trails and infrastructure in place. We decided to open a Haunted Hayride in October 1991. My friend, Jim Townsend, and I set up a 15-minute trail through the tall forest on the farm. My wife and business partner, Anne, sat at a picnic table taking admission money. New friends, Sam and Kurt Bonsall, helped with artwork and sets. Both acted in the show as well. Sam was at a hanging scene where we had two bodies hanging on either side of him, and he held the "hanging noose" behind his back. When that wagon came by, he could just pretend to be hanging, then jump out at the wagon. Great scare. Kurt hid behind a stump with an axe stuck in it. I remember driving the tractor when a lady on the ride said "look, an axe" I'm thinking jump now! And he did, scaring the heck out of her.

Looking back, it was very simple and would never survive in this day. With 25 friends and family, we operated this attraction for five nights. The trail was lit by tea candles placed in milk jugs and had to be constantly looked after. We had cut the tops off to allow easy access to the candles, however, the customers thought it would be funny to drop straw into them, starting a rash of small fires. That year, the hayride broke even, and my friends had a great time scaring the customers. In 1992, Mike Hearn stepped in. He's an HVAC guy and a blacksmith. We met when he came by to shoe my daughter's horse (she later became the headless horseman). Mike and I got talking and he said he could make pretty much anything burn. Thus started the Bates' love affair with pyrotechnics. Year 2 had us building some sets and adding new scenes. The hayride was still simple but was growing. One thing I have always loved is good music. I put myself through college by installing car sound systems. So with my electronic experience, we installed cassette decks on the tractors and recorded a movie-like soundtrack that set the tone for each scene. The beauty of this also worked as a timing mechanism so the tractor driver would go the same speed throughout the trail. It also puts the customer on edge and that allows our actors to easily scare them. Over the years the sound systems have become high tech, but the same timing applies. We now run 14 wagons and with this timing system we can run them 90 seconds apart, making every wagonload feels like they are the only one in the woods. They can't see the wagon in front or in back of them.

So my friend Mike decided to add fire to our witches' scene. With a huge, cast-iron kettle surrounded by stones in the shape of a pentagram, Mike built a system that, when activated, pumped propane into the bottom of the kettle that was filled with water. The top would start to bubble then burst into flames. The water caught fire. Meanwhile, my friend Ed Worrell acted as the Mummy. Now Ed was very particular about his part, and just about anything else. He came to my wife Anne and said he needed his costume repaired… it had some loose bandages. Of course, we all laughed at him. And so did the customers. He was called toilet paper man, and my favorite—Tampon man! Ed took it well. This was the year that we added the flying Dracula scene. We stretched a steel cable between two trees on opposite sides of the trail. Then add two drop cables in the center. We built platforms with ladders on each tree so the actor could climb down slowly, then fly over the wagon. It was an awesome scene. Kurt and Sam took turns flying. I remember when Kurt was on. He slowly climbed down the ladder, hissing and growling, dressed like Dracula. Some kid on the wagon yelled out "Hey, Dracula, you suck!" Kurt, not missing a beat, straightened up and yelled back just as he launched over the wagon "I suck BLOOD!" and he flew.

In 1990, my friend Ric Hatton and I started a burglar and fire alarm company. Logically, he also worked the hayride. With our electronics background, we were able to use alarm components to activate lights, sounds and animatronics in the show. The first couple of years the hayride averaged several thousand customers, but we were only charging two dollars per person. It was covering costs but not really making money. 1992 saw us working a deal with Halloween Adventure, a local mask and costume company that had about twenty stores. The owner gave us a two-thousand-dollar shopping spree in exchange for tickets to the hayride. This helped us get quality masks and costumes for the show. During these early years, I would walk the hayride trail making sure everyone was ok, and distributed beers to my friends. Of course, that would never work today.

Over the next couple of years, we raised our prices and added new, larger sets, and by 1995 our attendance reached twenty thousand customers. We were now making some bucks. We had developed our attraction in a total vacuum, not knowing about other attractions or haunted hayrides, and that made our ride unique.

In early 1996, I received an invitation to the Transworld Halloween trade show

in Chicago. I was a little skeptical at first but decided to attend. That was one of the best decisions we made. They had a huge convention center filled with animatronics, props, masks, makeup, costumes and everything related to the Halloween haunted attraction industry. They also had a series of seminars about how to open, operate and market attractions. I was ready to learn from the pillars of the Haunt community and grow my business. Leonard Pickle taught how to build a haunted house. Joe Jensen, who ran a huge haunt in Chicago, taught seminars. And I finally ended up taking a seminar on Haunted Hayrides. I'm sitting next to a guy

HARDWARE
WARE

who ran Charlie Brown's Christmas Tree Farm in Connecticut. He also did a haunted hayride using antique tractors. The fellow giving the seminar came on and started out by saying that they stopped running hayrides, and the best way to keep your customers happy was to throw crap at them. Things like small, plastic spiders, candy, and other "junk." Me, being forward, asked why he stopped doing hayrides. He told us the trucks kept getting stuck. I laughed and said to my friend "he's using trucks to pull his wagons." The guy giving the seminar heard me and said, "No, we didn't pull wagons." I was stunned. This guy was putting people in the bed of a pickup truck and calling it a hayride. At this point, I realized that we had a pretty good attraction and were ahead of most hayrides.

After taking Leonard's seminar on haunted houses and picking the heads of other haunt owners such as Joe Jensen and John Denley, I came home with plans to build my own haunted house; the Bates Motel was born. The first thing I did was contact my attorney to see if I could call it the Bates Motel. He checked for trademarks. Then he told me since it was my name, I could use it. In 2004 we trademarked Bates Motel, and it proved to be huge when Universal Studios tried to sue us in 2010 over their TV series of the same name. We came out on top.

So 1996 saw us build a 3500 square-foot "barn" that morphed into the Bates Motel. Our theory was to load customers into a side door and exit into our courtyard. This way, our hayride customers hanging out at the bonfires would see people come out screaming. It worked, but we had to give away a ton of free tickets to get people to start going through the house.

So in 1996, steps in Mark Grunwell. He worked for an electronic company that specialized in computer-controlled devices. Mark was instrumental in setting up the control system that operated the lighting, sound, and props in the haunted house. Working with Mark, we built wall panels, Sam and the build crew painted them, and we hired more actors and staff. My wife, Anne, ran the one-window ticket box office. After the opening weekend, I realized that we needed a bigger ticket booth. Along came Tyson Cooper, a good carpenter but lousy electronics guy. He had worked for a high-end sound company that provided huge sound systems for large concerts at stadiums around the country. Tyson and I were building out the new ticket booth around 2:00 am, pretty much in the bag, when a State Trooper stopped by. He wanted to make sure we weren't driving! This was our breakout year that put us squarely in the Haunt community. And along with Tyson came John Brady, who toured with Bon Jovi as a sound tech. He brought along his expertise with sound and lighting. Later, his wife Kelly would manage our concession stand.

Everything was going great. We were making money and paying bills. All staff were on payroll now, and we had several full-time guys working on the haunt. Then, Friday, September 28th, I got a notice from my Township. "You are in violation of your agricultural zoning. Cease and desist all attractions on your property." Now I'm freaking out as all our flyers have been put out, all radio marketing had started, staff were hired and placed, and they want me to shut down. We had spent tens of thousands of dollars getting ready, and if we shut down, it would ruin us. My friend and attorney, Dave Mallman, told me we had thirty days to appeal; go ahead and open, then try to get a zoning change in November. It worked. We had the best year to date, then set up a conditional use hearing with the board of supervisors in November. The board grilled me about the business, asking how many parking spaces we have, how many portable toilets, how many two-way radios, how many security staff and parking lot staff. I answered honestly and explained our operations. They then wrote an "Agritourism" ordinance that basically included everything I had told them. We were now legal in the Township.

1998 was a year of change. Mark Grunewll had a heart attack in February and told me he could not work that year. Around the same time, I became friends with Todd Beringer, who had just moved into the community and joined the fire company. Todd was the general manager for a very large bakery in Philadelphia and knew a lot about automation. He brought in another mechanical engineer named Nick Ostensacken, and between the two of them, cleaned up the wiring mess in the Bates Motel. Another newbie was Casey Grant. Casey worked for a disaster refurbishing business and was a very talented carpenter. Casey became our lead set builder, and our first real full-time employee.

The attractions kept growing with more sets, props and actors each year. New trails were constructed turning the 18-minute ride into a full 25 minutes. More tractors and wagons were added. Better sound equipment was installed, and the soundtrack was recorded in a professional sound studio owned by Bobby Zieglar. The 18' wagons were traded in for 24' wagons, and we added steps to a few of them.

In 2000, we decided to add a third attraction. This would be a walking trail in a corn field. We called it a corn maze, but it's really a trail where you cannot get lost. Some attractions do a haunted maze, but I wanted people to go through it as fast as possible. To me, throughput is essential to economic growth. So we cut the trail, built a couple of walk-through buildings, added scarecrows, and a sound system. That, along with 15 actors, cost us about $20,000. This attraction was a huge success with over 25,000 attending at $5 per ticket. This was also the year we began using online ticket sales. Back then it was a small percentage of our ticket sales. We also started getting sponsorships. The local Ford dealer became a large sponsor, and the Halloween Adventure shops were also sponsors.

In the middle of the 2000 haunt season, a new bar/restaurant opened 1/4 mile away. It immediately became our go to place after closing. Our customers all went there, and Duffer's Tavern was overwhelmed. We became great friends with Mike and Frank Slachta, the owners, and to this day we have an awesome relationship. We send them thousands of customers every September and October and they give us our employee appreciation party in November; four hours of buffet and open bar for over 350 people.

2001 was a strange year. After 9/11, many haunted attractions did not open. We decided to change some things and open, creating a charity for some of the victims. For the last several years, we had an animated hanging woman that would pop out from a second-floor balcony window and hang herself. This was like the nursemaid in the movie the Omen. This year, we kept the nightgown, added sandals, a turban and beard, and charged customers five bucks to hang Osama. All proceeds went to a friend whose husband died in tower two, and the wife of the pilot from flight 93, who lives nearby. The reaction was amazing, with people handing over twenties to push the button. We raised over $7,000.

This was also our best year to date as the weather was perfect. The only year with no rainouts. It was also a year of change. We stopped hosting bands because it kept people here longer, which caused the parking lot to overflow. We also stopped the bonfires for the same reason. We blamed the bonfire issue on the dry weather, and the bands on noise ordinance.

So now we had a great group of talented construction guys, artists, electricians and actor managers. We would attend the Transworld trade show and get ideas from other haunters and prop manufacturers. After collecting these ideas, we would sit down and start design work for the next season. Some of these people would come up with some cool ideas that may not be practical or cost effective. I would be the one to approve or knock down these ideas. Someone would come up with a new room in the Bates Motel. I would always ask "OK, where's the scare?" or "How can we build this, so it works 250 times a night for 30 nights?" Some guys would get upset if I didn't like their idea. One of them was Casey. He hated it when I shut him down, but I was the practical voice at the table.

Over the years we have had some great actors join our team. I remember one warm day in August when a young woman walked up the driveway. She told me that her parents had moved to Michigan, and she had lost her place to scare people on Halloween. She said her name was Alicia Newton, but everyone called her Harley. She also said that she had a two-headed calf in a jar. Wow! My kind of gal. I hired her on the spot. Harley was finishing up her 11th year of college at Penn University. Four years of pre-med vet school, four years Vet school, and three years of specialized school learning about all animals. She was a veterinarian that was going to specialize in Zoo animals as the coroner. She later worked for the Philadelphia Zoo, then the San Diego zoo, and finally as a vet for Disney. Harley talked about doing an autopsy on a full-size Rhino, using a chain saw. Harley Liked to fly. We had a flying rig over our hayride trail for many years, and that was the position she wanted. It's a tough spot as it chafes your body, but she loved it.

Another actor was Tim Cook. He insisted on running the chainsaw. He was there for over ten years before moving on. Dominic DiValerio was also another hit. Dominic would design and build his own rooms and costumes. One year he built an electric chair that was hinged to the floor. He'd activate the system with sound, fog, and strobe lights, then tilt forward and chase the customers. Another year we built a 13th Ghost room, and he was the Jackal. Dominic built the head cage himself. Dom was funny because his daytime job was as an optician. He used to say that he had to be nice to customers for 11 months, then, with unrecognizable masks or makeup, scare the hell out of them in October.

In 2004, I helped form a Haunt group called America Haunts. It started as five of the larger haunted attractions across the country. We would meet and exchange ideas, make group buys and promote our attractions. Over the next four years we added several more members. It is an invitation only group and there are specific criteria to be a member. This was around the time when Bates Motel started making the top 13 lists. It's exciting to see your attraction listed in the Wall Street journal or CNN Travel. We were getting noticed on a national level. Also, around this time, a young guy named John Walsh came on as an actor in the haunted Trail. His mother, Thelma was an actress and his stepdad, Charlie Conrad managed the trail. John later took over as the IT guy and really put us on the cutting edge. John still works here managing the Haunted Trail as well as keeping our internet and sound systems operational. Last year, we added 72 HD cameras, a server, and a complete sound system throughout the entire property. John also set up our point-of-sale system and Photo Touch camera systems where customers can buy photos of themselves.

This was also the same time that some of my children began working for us. My older son, Drew, brought in several of his Scout buddies, who worked as actors in the hayride. My daughter, Angela, worked in Human resources, hiring staff and managing actor placement. Daughter, Katie, acted as the headless horseman for several years. Daughter, Veronica, acted in the hayride and then helped in the concession stand, and younger son, Ben, was an actor fill-in, going to different scenes as needed. Our youngest daughter, Diana, would go on to manage our escape rooms and Laser-tag facility. My wife, Anne, still handles all the finances; bills, payroll, bank accounts, etc., however, Veronica is being groomed to take over this aspect of the business.

In 2006, A couple of brothers stopped by in August and said they wanted to work for us. They live in North Philadelphia, about an hour away. They said they had worked for another haunt called Scare Brothers, but they wanted to work here. I asked why, and they said they thought we were the best in the area and that their old employers didn't give them the resources to do a professional job. I called Scare Brothers, and they said that these guys couldn't finish a job on time. So, I decided to give them a shot. Shawn and Rob Sieger became a huge part of our business over the years. Both still work here today as makeup artists and set designers. This was also the year that I fired Casey. That summer, about twelve of my hayride actors said they weren't coming back. I wanted to know why. One guy told me that the last year, Casey had been a terrible manager, and they didn't want to work under him. Since he only knew carpentry, I told him if something wooden breaks, fix it. I then put my son Ben in charge of the hayride. All those actors came back, and they were more than happy with the change. At the end of the season, it was obvious that Casey needed to go. Shawn and Rob were amazed that I had just fired our construction manager. A month later, Chris Malloy showed up. He was an out of work machinist and a good carpenter. He stepped right into Casey's position, running the build crew and managing the hayride. Our attraction got better because of that. It seemed that whatever the reason, when one manager left, another person would show up and improve our team.

As the years went by, the attractions became more intricate, more realistic and more expensive. In 2010, Ben graduated from Universal Technical Institutes with degrees in Auto mechanics, Diesel mechanics, and hydraulics. In his cap and gown, Ben told us he wanted to work for the company. He came on full-time as the build crew manager and has done an outstanding job. The great thing about having a mechanic on staff is that he can service the tractors and wagons. Ben also began building custom animatronic props while Shawn, Cosimo, and the rest of the art team would decorate them.

In 2012, we hired Interactive Ticketing to run our online sales. I had contacted several online ticketing companies, but IT gave me the best deal. I soon became friends with the owners, Dave

Arevello and Terry Howisey. Both guys were from Sacramento and were big time into wine. They gave us a great deal, and we've been using them ever since.

Over the many years that we have been in business, customers and staff have gotten engaged and married on the farm. One guy called me in May and wanted to set up a date to ask his girlfriend to marry him. It was all planned out. We were going to do the deed in the haunted trails mausoleum. The guy brought his girl and another couple that was in on the deal. They were let into the trail by themselves, then the next group was held up for several minutes. When they entered the mausoleum, the doors closed, and they were trapped. One actor came out with a shotgun (non-firing), kicked the guy behind his knee, forcing him to kneel. Pointing the gun at this fellow's head, Shawn yelled, "You got something to say, boy." The second actress, who flies overhead, spun over and dropped the box with the ring. He proposed and she said yes, although she was shaking with fear! Fortunately, we had a film crew there and they got it all on tape. If you want to see it, go to YouTube and search Bates Motel wedding proposal.

Other people who met here were Mike Sankevitch and Little Ann. He oversaw the parking lot, and Ann ran the concession stand. They met here, and a few years later married and moved to South Carolina. Before that, Cousin Bill Bruce and wife Margaret worked parking and concessions.

For several years, things were cranking along. Good friends, good seasons and a lot of satisfied customers. I concentrated more on the marketing end of the business, Ben and the build crew were banging out new additions, and my wife Anne was tackling the tough job of CFO, chief financial officer, paying bills, running payroll and everything else in between.

Then in 2019, Chris Malloy retired due to severe arthritis in his hands and feet. He was just 50 years old but couldn't stand for more than fifteen minutes. In comes Chris Knight, my new son-in-law. Chris married Daughter Diana and they now have three children. Chris was another upgrade as he had lots of experience in construction, metal work, and electrical works. Diana was a huge part of the business, helping in the concession stand and managing the Escape Room and Laser Tag business that Ben and I started in

2016. So 2019 was one of the best years to date, with over 50,000 customers attending.

Many seasons had issues. Traffic jams and full parking lots were a big problem. Neighbors complained, and State Troopers would ask us to close the lots when the traffic hit one-hour backups. 2020 solved all these problems. March 13, 2020 was the beginning of the Covid-19 lockdown. Everything stopped. Our escape rooms were closed for five months. We had no idea if the hayride could open that year. Transworld was cancelled. We shut down all-new set construction and laid off full-time employees. Everything shut down. In mid-August, our governor came out and said if there are outdoor events, they could open, provided there were a maximum of 5 people per one thousand square feet of space. Hell, we had eighty-two acres! I could host thousands.

So, this is how we delt with Covid. First, we went to all timed ticketing and only online sales. This alleviated the traffic and parking issues. We went to a one price for all three attractions. This increased income as we eliminated child tickets, a la carte tickets, and changed to a linear show. We set up a security checkpoint where everyone was funneled to. Customers went through metal detectors operated by off duty Sheriffs who did this at the court-house. Customers had their temperature taken, then moved into queue lines that were doubled in size to allow social distancing. Red tape was added to the rope in the queue in six-foot inter-vals. Hand sanitizers were everywhere. Customers were asked to wear masks. All actors and staff wore masks. This eliminated the makeup costs and staff, saving more money. Actors were trained to stay back from customers. Since you can't socially distance on a hay wagon, we changed the hayride into a walking trail. Funny thing was that when we ran the hayride, it took about twenty-six minutes. When the customers walked the trail, it took them six-teen minutes. Since we were utilizing timed ticketing, we were able keep the queue lines down to a minimum. Some customers who were out of shape needed help going up the hills at the end of the trail. So, we had an EMT staff manning the hill with a golf cart. Chris Knight found a street sign that read "Asthma Hill" and proudly hung it from a tree at the bottom of the hill.

2020 saw us go to a linear format. Customers went through

RESTLESS SOULS CE

the screening, walked the hayride trail, went through the Revenge of the Scarecrows haunted trail, and then into the Bates Motel. We limited the concession stand to simple food and removed the picnic tables, basically forcing customers to get something to eat, then leave the property. In the past, Friday nights were kiddie city. Parents would drop off teens and come back for them around 11:00 pm. Covid put a stop to that. We told the kids they had to call for a ride or leave the property. All these things made our business much more efficient. More income, more profit, fewer staff and less payroll all added up to 2020 being the best year to date. This was also the year that CNN Travel named us the number one haunted attraction in America.

2021 was just another repeat of 2020. Same setup, same ticketing, same walking trail. More customers. This year, America Haunts named us as the most entertaining haunted attraction in the country. This brought out a frenzy of local and national media. Every TV station in Philadelphia came out for live segments, interviews and background videos, CBS, ABC, NBC, Fox news, and more all showed off the Bates Motel that year. And this made 2021 the best year to date; even better than 2020.

Over the last two years we didn't make many changes to the hayride trail. 2021 saw us refurbish seven rooms in the Bates Motel, which took many months. In 2022 our team decided to make big changes to the hayride. This was the year that we hired Dewey. He's a young guy with good construction experience. His real name is Evan, but when you work for Ben, you always get a nickname. Dewey's name was derived from another guy who had worked here the year before. Evan Dumont worked for a couple years. So, we couldn't call him Evan, and Dumont was nicknamed by his last name, therefore the new Evan became Dumont, then shortened to Dewey. Also, at this time we hired Gianna full-time to run the art department. She had been working for us for ten years as an actress and makeup artist. Gianna was instrumental in decorating and painting the new rooms in the Bates Motel and the new western scene.

As Covid was winding down, we decided to bring back the Hayride. This was the main attraction here, and customers wanted to ride again. We started by rebuilding the hayride entrance, the castle scene. A neighbor had a bunch of 35' Steel lamp posts used in parking lots. Another friend up north had access to thousands of feet of chain link fencing that was removed from tennis courts. We have our own commercial spray foam machine used to insulate buildings. So the build team made the huge castle that you see in the photos. Along with the castle, we decided to build a western town. Back in the '90s we had a western village that had some great scares and details. That was abandoned when the asylum scene was built. Cosimo designed the buildings, and with Gianna and Dewey, it came to life. Wanting to add some realism, I went overboard buying covered wagons and stagecoaches from the Amish in Lancaster, PA. Full-size horses and steers were purchased from Texas and installed throughout the scene. There's a lot of inside jokes throughout our attractions; ones that only we know. Cos decided to name the stores and buildings after my in-laws. For example, Minacci Brothers Gun shop. The second building in this scene is a two-story hotel and saloon. Before construction, we had a film crew shooting a commercial. So we set up a saloon scene in Ben's shop and shot a thirty second bar fight scene, with pretty saloon gals and a bunch of cowboys. We even had Dave Davis swinging one handed from a wagon-wheel chandelier with a beer in his hand. After building the scene, we added scrim to the downstairs windows and to the second-floor window. Then we projected the videos of Dave swinging on the second floor and the bar fight on the first-floor windows. It worked out better than I could have hoped for.

2022 saw us bringing back the hayride and adding a lot of new actors and staff. Covid was about over, and customers came out in large numbers. The changes that we implemented stayed in place except for the social distancing and mask wearing. Makeup came back, and actors could go after the customers again. This turned out to be the best season ever and our team is already working hard on new additions for 2023.

FIELD OF SCREAMS

FIELD OF SCREAMS: GENE & JIM SCHOPF

GENE

Gene Schopf's passion for entrepreneurship started from an early age peddling homegrown vegetables around his neighborhood. Spending much of his younger years doing agricultural work on his family farm, he was taught the value of working hard. He proved this in his hobbies as well; Gene was a very talented wrestler during his high school and college careers and even ranked 12th in the nation as a Division I Collegiate wrestler. This drive motivated him to partner with his brother to open a roadside market at his childhood home where they could sell the produce that they raised on their farm. He did this all while attending Millersville University to earn a degree in secondary education. After graduating from college in 1989, he taught Technology Education at three schools before settling into Conestoga Valley High School from 1992 – 2003. Gene married his wife Sandy in 1992, and they had three children: Kyle, Kerri, and Tanner. He then went on to earn his master's degree in education from Gratz College in 1999. Just after Gene began his teaching career, he and his brother Jim created Field of Screams in 1993 on their family farm in Mountville, PA. Gene retired from teaching in early 2004 and made Field of Screams his full-time career. After years of dedication and perseverance, Field of Screams has become a world-class haunt. Gene still uses his technology education skills in his role at Field of Screams. He oversees the amazing set design and construction crew, and is hands-on when it comes to creating incomparable props and scenes. He is passionate about the creation process. Field of Screams has been commended on their ability to fully immerse patrons into the ultimate atmosFEAR of Halloween! They have been named the #1 haunted attraction from USA Today and have been featured on Discovery's Travel Channel, *The Howard Stern Show, Oprah* magazine, and *Time* magazine. Gene's passion for the haunt industry is clear through his creations. He served on the Board of Directors for the Haunted Attraction Association (HAA), serving as Vice-President from 2010 – 2012. Gene was also instrumental in working with the PA Department of Agriculture in forming safety regulations and an inspector's safety test for haunted houses across the state of Pennsylvania. This dedication of Field of Screams to the haunt industry was honored in 2015 when they received the Board of Directors Award from the Haunted Attraction Association. Gene remains devoted to the art of the scare and will continue to harvest fears for many years to come.

JIM

im is the younger Schopf brother by six years, so he has always admired his older brother, Gene. Their comradery grew especially close when they became business partners when Jim was just a sixth grader. The brothers raised and peddled their own produce, and operated a roadside stand while Gene was in college and Jim was still in junior high school. Jim had to keep up with his older brother, and the same quality of hard work was instilled in him through farming and wrestling. Jim was a top wrestler during high school and college. During his senior year in college, Jim was chosen as Athlete of the Year at Millersville University, and competed in the NCAA Division I National Championships, where he finished in the top 12. In 1993, he and his brother expanded their farming operation and created Field of Screams. After graduating from college in 1995 with a degree in secondary education, Jim taught mathematics at Lampeter Strasburg High School, and married his wife, Andrea, in 2000. They have two children, Sydney and Sutton. He earned his master's degree in education from Gratz College in 2003. Jim retired from teaching in the summer of 2003 to put all his focus into advancing Field of Screams and Schopf Bros. Farms. Jim oversees Schopf Bros, LLC and handles all the farming for the business, as well as the seasonal activities such as Easter flowers, produce, pumpkins, and Christmas trees. Jim also manages the Field of Screams office staff, and handles all the marketing, sponsorships, and financial aspects of the business. Jim has a knack for forming long-standing promotional partnerships with both local businesses as well as national chains. He also oversees the public relations for Field of Screams and has developed a large network of relationships. He works directly with local and national press outlets in the promotion of the Field of Screams event every year. Through these efforts, Field of Screams has become a household name in the tri-state area. Additionally, patrons from all over the world come to Field of Screams to Experience the Chill. From 2015 – 2020, Jim was a vital part of creating the set of ASTM safety standards for hayrides that is now used across the country. Jim has a great passion for the haunt industry, the people in it, and will continue to share his love of scaring for many years to come.

Gene: We've come a long way from the beginning of Field of Screams. It was so different then—it used to be that we designed a skit and built it on the fly. We'd say, "let's have a troll scene," and we'd mow a spot in the cornfield, put a stump there, and throw rice up in the air as we were pretending to eat the guts of a victim. Then when a wagon came, we'd run at it. Old skits involved whatever we had around laying around the farm—you used what you had because there was no money! Luckily, this quickly changed, and obviously as years progressed, we got more sophisticated. We now work on a three-year build schedule, meaning every scene is planned three years in advance, and many times these builds are in several stages. Our builds try to incorporate all of the senses. In the outdoor skits we include fire, smell, and water effects, and we want to have so many pneumatics and so much action that even if there were no actors, it would be a great, scary scene. We involve our entire construction crew as part of the planning process. We research scenes, gather and store props, parts, and scenic decor several years ahead of time. This way, when that build is on the schedule, we already have everything we need. We try to build almost all props in-house; sometimes, however, it makes more sense to purchase certain items, as building one-offs or large props may be cost prohibitive. Hayride scenes are the biggest and most elaborate as far as sets go because they are so immense—we need to cover such a huge area. One of our Hayride scenes is 100' long, 20' tall, and 50' wide on both sides of the wagon. A scene like this is almost like building an entire haunted house! Our goal is to play on people's fears, but we try to keep a loose, broad theme so you are not locked into one particular idea. We do strive to have some congruity between scenes. All of our attractions see major changes every year. Obviously, even with the best-made plans and all this in place, things still happen and change. I've discovered that the easiest way to save time in your build schedule is to just cross off the start date next to the item and put the following year after it—now you've just saved months of work!

Jim: There are a lot of elements to consider when designing a horror experience for guests. First and foremost, you need to consider how you are going to get the most impact and thrill out of the experience. When we think about creating a scene in a haunted attraction there are many elements to consider. To deliver the best impact, you need to think about incorporating as many of the five senses as possible. The visual impact is probably the most important, so the experience needs to look horrific or threatening. The next goal is to incorporate an authentic sound to help sell the reality of the experience. This would include whatever sound or skit lines that a performer may be making, as well as natural background and ambient sounds. Incorporating a scent into the experience as well will subliminally give the scene an authentic reality. The senses of feel and taste can also be included by creating an environment where participants are in close quarters to the scene, and if the scent of the scene is pulled off perfectly, the guest can even "taste" the fear!

Secondly, after perfecting the ultimate scene described above, there are many other factors to consider. The scene must have the proper guest flow for effective throughput, scare value, and safety. The actor's hiding spot or "acting area" must be properly positioned and integrated in order to achieve the optimum scare impact, along with providing the performer a way to quickly retreat and reset for the next group of victims. Additionally, considering the entertainment value of the scene is important for those quests who are less likely to be terrified but will find value and enjoyment in the immense details, set design, quality of construction, and authenticity of the experience. The attention to detail in a scene is vitally important in a haunted attraction, because it gives repeat

customers the perception that you are constantly changing a scene around when they see things in the scene that they haven't noticed in prior visits. And then, of course, there is the safety consideration to ensure that the setting is a safe environment for both the guest and the performer.

Lastly, the look of the performer in the scene must be completely authentic, from head to toe, in order to give it the final stamp of approval! The performer must fully immerse themselves in becoming the character that they are portraying through their costume, skit lines, characteristics, and mannerisms.

WHEN IS THE LAST TIME YOU WERE GENUINELY SCARED BY SOMETHING SOMEONE CREATED?

Jim: Being a lover of haunted attractions and running a professional haunted attraction for over three decades, I cannot even remember the last time I was genuinely scared! However, what gets me the most are real threats, such as a vicious dog, a slithering snake, or venomous spiders. And then, of course, the dark and the unknown are good psychological thrills!

Gene: When God creates rain in October, it scares me! The only things I'm really afraid of are needles and rain in October!

WHAT IS THE INSPIRATION FOR THE SCARES/SKITS/IDEAS FOR WHAT YOU CREATE AT FOS?

Gene: I get inspiration from being passionate about creating, designing, and building. The payoff is spending a year creating something, and then tens of thousands of people come out and enjoy it and say how much they like it. My inspiration is a satisfied customer.

Jim: The creations at Field of Screams are a collaboration of ideas from our experienced team of Fright Engineers. We start with a simple concept of a broad theme for a particular scene, skit, or scare, and then brainstorm concepts around those ideas. With our experienced team of professionals giving input, we are able to quickly hone-in on the ultimate idea. This idea will continue to morph as it evolves in our minds, and even as we are constructing, we occasionally will make modifications. Sometimes the scenes are designed around a particular scare that we think may be new and creative and amazing, and sometimes the scenes are designed around a theme that we feel will create an intimidating and terrifying environment. Occasionally a scene is created around a particular character that we feel would provide the perfect menacing experience at Field of Screams.

WHAT DO YOU LOVE ABOUT THE GENRE OF HORROR?

Gene: What I love about the horror genre is that anybody can be anything they want to be. It produces an opportunity for kids and adults to just let loose and have fun. You can dress up and create any character that you can imagine. Halloween is a fun holiday to scare and be scared.

Jim: What I love most about the genre of horror is that it can encompass many different forms. There are so many ways and situations to scare people. The amazing part of a haunted attraction is that the patron is literally an active participant in the horror scenario, and not just watching it on a screen. They are in the real-life horror setting! This scene can encompass many different forms. You can have a kitchen with a Mad Chef, or you can have a dentist office with a demented dentist. You can have a garage with a maniacal mechanic. You can creep people out, you can gore people out, you can freak people out, and so on! The options are limitless!

DO YOU HAVE ANY INFLUENCES FOR YOUR CREATIONS?

Jim: I consider everything in my life as an influence for my Haunted creations. Wherever I am, I observe what frightens people. I observe mannerisms and behaviors, and I am constantly thinking about that person in a haunted attraction, and what would scare them. If I see decorations, I automatically think of how that would look as haunted décor. I turn the normal things in everyday life into the absolutely horrific! Everything I create in the horror realm I try to make as authentic as possible so that it's not a re-creation of anything else that I have seen directly.

Gene: I think your influences are your customers and their reactions, your team, and the trade shows like Transworld and IAPPA. And of course, all the crazy stuff that lives in your head!

WHAT IS YOUR FAVORITE HALLOWEEN TREAT?

Gene: Pumpkin spiced coffee!

Jim: If we are talking about food, then being from the Amish heartland of Lancaster County, I'd enjoy a moist pumpkin Whoopie pie! For those outside of Amish country, you may need to Google that.

DESCRIBE THE PERFECT HALLOWEEN.

Jim: My perfect Halloween is being at Field of Screams on a dark night with a misty fog settling in over the complex. Cars are starting to pour in. Patrons are getting out of their cars—some with reservation, some with excitement, and some already scared out of their minds in anticipation of what is about to come. Then seeing these guests experience the haunted attractions that our team has brought to life is a Halloween treat like no other! Hearing the shrieks, the screams, the laughter, and sometimes seeing the tears is the best Halloween ever!

Gene: My Perfect Halloween: 60 degrees, full moon, and a packed crowd at Field of Screams!

FIELD
OF
SCREAMS
ENTER

A SPOTLIGHT ON ONE OF AMERICA'S PREMIER HAUNTED ATTRACTIONS

ield of Screams is America's leading Haunted Attraction and consists of four horrifying events: The Haunted Hayride, a 25-minute tractor-pulled hayride through the cornfield; The Den of Darkness, a 5,000 square foot Haunted Mansion-style walkthrough attraction; The Frightmare Asylum, a 6,000 square foot Haunted Hospital-style walkthrough attraction; and Nocturnal Wasteland, a 20-minute haunted walk through the woods. With additional nightly entertainment, special events, games, and a large selection of food, Field of Screams is the ultimate Haunted Amusement Park. Situated on a 35-acre family farm in rural south-central Pennsylvania, Field of Screams is centrally located to several major cities, including Philadelphia, Baltimore, and New York.

THE BEGINNING

The owners of Field of Screams, brothers Gene and Jim Schopf, originally had no intention of creating a full-time haunted attraction, let alone creating one of the largest full-time haunted attractions in the country! They grew up in a house bordering the property of their family farm in Mountville, PA—an ideal setting of country farmland just outside the growing city of Lancaster, PA.

Their father was an elementary school teacher and raised produce and vegetables, while also raising chickens. The family had other farm animals such as cows, sheep, ducks, and geese in the barn that now houses the Den of Darkness. The boys grew up living the traditional "farm life"—going to Sunday dinner at their grandmother's farmhouse and working with the crops as early as sorting potatoes in the potato cellar at four years old! As Gene entered seventh grade, he began selling the family's homegrown vegetables to his neighbors. The entrepreneurial bug bit early, and Gene and Jim became business partners in 1984 when Gene was a senior in high school and Jim was in the sixth grade. They continued peddling their homegrown produce by pulling their wagon of goods door-to-door; although once partners, the peddling became Jim's job because Gene thought his younger brother was cuter and sweeter and would sell more to their elderly neighbors! As produce sales increased, the boys set up a small roadside stand in the front yard of their parents' house. They raised sugar peas, spring onions, rhubarb, cantaloupes, watermelons, sweet corn, pumpkins, and almost anything else you could imagine. The brothers also learned valuable hard work and discipline lessons from both farming and sports—particularly wrestling, which both boys began with earnest in elementary school.

Although they were expected to work hard on the farm, Gene and Jim did enjoy a little fun as well. Their mother always loved Halloween and enjoyed dressing her kids in costumes and taking them trick-or-treating. She would often purchase the old-style plastic masks with the single white elastic strap, and then piece together the rest of the costume out of homemade components. The kids looked forward to this holiday every year. The Schopfs did not have a television in their house until 1987, so Gene and Jim did not have the traditional influences most haunters have of watching horror movies while growing up. Instead, they regularly visited a Haunted Attraction operated by their local Youth for Christ Center called Scream in the Dark. This was a fundraiser for the local church youth group and was also used as an outreach tool to the community. Gene and Jim frequented this attraction several times each year and loved being scared by the goblins. They imagined that dressing up as a character in the haunted house who was able to jump out and scare people would be an incredible amount of fun. When the Scream in the Dark attraction closed its doors in 1983, the boys thought about how amazing it would be to develop a similar experience for people to enjoy. They had the opportunity to do this just a year or two later, when they used one of the old barns on the farm to create their own haunted barn, complete with a scary straw bale maze. They had a few homemade props but relied heavily on the creepiness of the old barn itself to add the element of fear. Many local scout troops and youth groups visited the farm for this experience, complete with their mom serving apple cider and gingersnap cookies at the end. While they did not charge for the groups to go through the barn, Gene and Jim got a thrill from having people be scared of something they created.

Their homespun haunted barn only lasted a couple of years, but Gene and Jim continued their produce operations as Gene attended college at Millersville University and Jim completed high school. Gene graduated from MU with a Bachelor of Science in Education, and he and his wife purchased their own farm just a few miles from the family farm in Mountville. This location enabled the brothers to set up a large roadside market and gave them an additional 20 acres of land on which to grow their crops. They continued their father's tradition of raising started capons (neutered roosters). They purchased male peeps from the hatchery at one day old, and when the birds were 2 ½ weeks old, they performed the surgical process of castrating them. Gene and Jim became known across several states for their speed and accuracy in caponizing—at their peak they could caponize 250 birds in one hour! They also expanded their roadside stand into multiple seasons, including Easter and Mother's Day with flowers, produce, pumpkins, and Christmas trees. To enhance the experience of customers purchasing pumpkins in the fall, they began to offer non-scary hayrides to their pumpkin patches and realized how much people enjoyed the tractor-pulled hayride. They also remembered how much fun their experiences at Scream in the Dark were, and they began to think about creating a scary hayride.

THE EARLY STAGES

The idea of a haunted hayride came to fruition in 1993 when Schopf Bros Farms converted its pumpkin patch wagon into its first Field of Screams haunted hayride wagon. September of 1993 marks the date when the Schopf Bros expanded from not only producing crops but also to harvesting fear! Gene and Jim created this hayride solely to have fun scaring people, with no knowledge of what to expect from their first year in operation. Their first skits had very generic scenes and props, and Gene and Jim operated most of the skits themselves. Since there was only one wagon in operation, they would often act at one skit and change costumes while running ahead to the next skit. They had a few of their friends pose as actors and made changes as they went. There was no marketing plan in year one, and very little planning. Most of the items used in their skits were found lying around the farm, as there was also essentially no budget to make purchases. Despite the low budget and lack of special effects, to their amazement 3,000 customers loved the thrill of being scared while riding a tractor-pulled wagon deep into a field towering with swaying rows of corn.

The second year of Field of Screams brought a small marketing plan involving posters and brochures placed at local stores, revamped scenes in the hayride with additional actors, and double the attendance from the first year. The parking lot for the first two years was a pasture in between the hayride and the two barns on the property that housed the family's farm animals. As the second season ended, the brothers realized that this small 1/4 acre lot holding 50 cars would no longer be sufficient. They made plans to convert one of their sweet corn fields into a larger parking lot for season three.

As the summer of 1995 rolled around, Jim also graduated from Millerville University with a Bachelor of Science degree in Education. Although both brothers were teaching at local high schools in their respective fields, they wanted to expand this haunted attraction hobby to include a haunted house. They decided to use the barn that had housed their scary straw maze ten years earlier and spent the summer converting it into the Den of Darkness. Existing partitions as well as new walls created rooms,

hallways, and mazes for a three-story barn of terror. The areas in the Den are ideal for an up-close and personal scare unique to almost every patron, and the original character of the barn still plays an important role as part of the aesthetics.

GROWING YEARS

The next major addition for Field of Screams debuted in 2002, when Gene and Jim decided to convert the chicken house/potato cellar on the property into a very unique four-story, 3-D Haunted House called the 3-D Frightmare. Construction on this building began as soon as the 2001 season ended. The entire inside of the building was gutted, and the Schopfs essentially built a barn within the original structure. Gene qualified for a sabbatical from his teaching job during the 2001 – 2002 school year and was therefore able to spend extra time building the interior of this haunt in between trips with his family. Once the structure was completed, Field of Screams brought in Stuart Smith of Stuartizm Designs to paint the entire building in 3D effects. The result was an eye-popping display of color, enhanced by Chromadepth 3-D glasses. This haunt remained in place for five years, but in being consistent with their desire to change and create new scares and effects, in 2007 Gene and Jim evolved this attraction into the Frightmare Asylum. The result was a move from the bright lights of the 3-D experience to a darker and scarier haunted hospital. The Asylum is an intense walkthrough experience that depicts many scenes that a person would have actually seen in an insane asylum in the early 1900s.

As the years passed, the attendance at Field of Screams continued to grow, and the attraction was quickly becoming a leader in the haunt industry by providing high-quality sets and scenic designs as well as effective scares. The Schopfs were finding it difficult to teach at local high schools during the day, work full-time on Field of Screams during the evenings and on weekends, and still find time for their young families. By this time, Gene and his wife had three children, and Jim and his wife had purchased their own farm and were expecting their first child. During the 2003 – 2004 school year, both Gene and Jim had the opportunity to retire early from teaching. Despite the success of both Field of Screams and their farming operation, it took a leap of faith to leave the security of teaching jobs to live the dream of working full-time in their own business. The brothers were always driven to work hard. They developed a strong work ethic at an early age while tending to crops and animals on the family farm, as well as both boys being Division I Collegiate wrestlers. As wrestlers, the grit and determination of competing at such a high level helped drive them as they went full steam ahead.

Over the next several years, Field of Screams gained in popularity. Gene and Jim continued to advance and improve their attractions with the most up-to-date technology and increasingly complex set designs. They work on prop construction and scenic changes year-round. Jim insists, "You have to change to stay ahead of the curve. People don't want to come back year after year and see the same scares. By changing some of the skits each year, customers never know what to expect. They do know that they can expect something different than the last time they came." While they use several pneumatics in their haunted attractions, Gene and Jim prefer to use as many live actor scares as possible, and never substitute pneumatics for a live scare. Gene says, "Nothing beats a real person flying out and providing a quality scare! Pneumatics can get some good scares and can serve as eye candy, but a real person is the best!" In 2013 Field of Screams introduced its fourth attraction, Nocturnal Wasteland. This is an action-packed, 20-minute outdoor attraction where guests walk through an old section of woods on the Field of Screams property. This attraction was conceptualized for years, and the original plan was to build it over a full year and introduce it in 2014. Once construction began, however, excitement and drive overruled, and the newest attraction was built in one intense summer by Gene, Jim, and their full-time construction and design team. The trail consists of different actor-driven scenes placed along a pathway buried in the dark woods. Those brave enough to venture along this course will encounter truly unique features, such as a catwalk that suspends them in the air high above the hayride. Since its inception, the Nocturnal Wasteland has been constantly upgraded, and there is always something new each year for customers to experience, just like with the other three attractions on the property. Another 2013 addition to Field of Screams was a 5K Zombie Fun Run. Patterned after the popular mud runs and warrior courses, runners have the opportunity to race along a path through the attractions at Field of Screams while also completing challenging obstacles. They wear a flag football belt holding three flags, which represent three lives. The runners' goal is to complete the course "alive," which means avoiding the zombies found in the zombie zones, where a crazed zombie tries to attack and steal a life. As long as a runner has at least one flag at the end of the 5K course, they have "survived." If no flags remain, the runner has become "infected." Either way, the runner completes the race and receives a medal accordingly! This fun run proved popular for people of all ages, as Field of Screams offers day waves, night waves, and waves specifically designed for younger children.

In 2016, Field of Screams began to offer an Extreme Blackout night which has traditionally been held in November on the last night of their regular season. This one night allows the actors in the attractions to interact with customers in a more intense manner than normal. Those brave enough to experience Extreme Blackout are forced to succumb to extreme methods of torture as they venture through all four of the attractions. Gene and Jim designed detailed scenarios for certain scenes in each attraction and trained specific actors in how to execute their torture methods safely, while also terrorizing victims. Each participating customer must sign a release waiver and receive rules (including a safe word) from the security staff on site. While this type of intense scare is not for all customers, Gene and Jim have discovered that there is a niche for those who truly enjoy the extreme level of fear!

PRESENT DAY (2023)

Each year the attendance at Field of Screams has grown, and this small hobby quickly expanded into one of the top haunts in the nation. Continuously improving scenes and developing new ones, along with providing engaging additional activities that customers can enjoy while onsite, keeps legions of Field of Screams fans returning each year.

The epicenter of Field of Screams is the massive Entertainment Area, a location where fun and exciting activities and entertainment

FOX 43
NEWS
FIELD OF SCREAMS

are always happening. This area is brightly lit and is jam-packed with action. If you are hungry, this is the place to be, with food vendors serving everything from pulled pork sandwiches and pit beef platters to pizza and funnel cakes. The massive Scream Shop, which sells Field of Screams branded souvenirs and Halloween merchandise, has items such as t-shirts, hats, sweatshirts and custom jackets. The entertainment area also boasts a stage for live entertainment, spooky-themed carnival games, axe throwing, mini escape rooms, a beer garden, and multiple photo ops. If you are too scared to enter the attractions, you'll surely be entertained and amused while you wait! In 2022, to commemorate their 30th anniversary, Field of Screams introduced an elaborate and immersive light, sound, and 3-D mapping projection show in the entertainment area. In this presentation, characters and graphics are projected onto both the Asylum and the Den to create an entertaining display that brings the exteriors of these buildings to life every 30 minutes.

Beginning in 2019, Field of Screams added four off-season events to their schedule. These include one-evening haunts for Christmas, Valentine's Day, St. Patrick's Day, and a Halfway to Halloween event in May. The Den and Asylum haunted houses are open for each of these events. While the heart of the scares and scenes remains the same as during the regular season, the décor changes based on the holiday. The design team incorporates holiday-themed decorations throughout both haunted houses and the entertainment area. At Christmas, amid hundreds of strands of Christmas lights, they focus on creepy Santas, demented elves, and rogue reindeer. For Valentine's Day, lights become white, pink, and red, and thousands of hearts highlight the theme of romance gone wrong with crazed Cupid. St. Patrick's Day focuses on lunatic leprechauns and terrifying trolls and the havoc they wreak throughout the scenes. Halfway to Halloween returns to regular sets and creates anticipation for the full show in the fall.Field of Screams is a labor of love for Gene and Jim, and they are the driving forces behind the haunt—they want to provide the best haunted experience possible for their patrons. After they spent about five years in the haunting business, Jim and Gene began to visit numerous trade shows and attend many seminars to gather information about the industry. They still enjoy visiting other haunted attractions, both in their area during the season, as well as haunts all over the country in the off-season. These visits can be in the capacity of an educational tour of another attraction, or they are for consulting purposes, when a haunt is ready to take their attraction to the next level. While they enjoy viewing and taking inspiration from props that large companies have designed, Gene and Jim often prefer to build their own variations of what they see. This enables Field of Screams to present a custom-designed show and offer a unique experience that patrons will be hard-pressed to find elsewhere. Field of Screams is a year-round project and requires work every day. The brothers are proud to have a dedicated team of employees who are as driven as they are when it comes to improving Field of Screams and enhancing the haunted experience from one year to the next. They have a full-time crew of twelve people in addition to themselves who work year-round on creating, building, designing, managing, and marketing. Two of these employees are Gene's sons, who joined the business after college. Jim's kids are still completing school, and work in the business during busy seasons.During the haunt season, Field of Screams has over 200 crew members to make sure guests receive the scare of their lives each night. Gene and Jim appreciate every member of their team, from the parking attendants to the actors in the buildings—each person has an important role in the operation of the event. Field of Screams is also heavily involved in local non-profit organizations and charities. One of the largest charities they work with is the Ronald McDonald House. Working with this group for the last 15 years has proved to be very rewarding for the Schopfs, who have donated over $140,000 to this organization. The PA Breast Cancer Coalition is the lead beneficiary for the Zombie Fun Run, and Field of Screams also is heavily involved with the Rutter's Children's Charities, among many other local associations. Giving back to their community has become an essential part of their business.

Here is a current look at what the four attractions have become as of the publishing of this book:

THE HAUNTED HAYRIDE

The original Hayride began as a one-wagon operation, but today consists of 11 tractors pulling wagons that are 35' long, 9' wide and hold upwards of 80 people. The tractors are from the 1970's and are still used on the family farms, while the wagons were custom-built by an Amishman and are complete with a custom surround-sound system installed by the Field of Screams team. A reporter from *Millersville University's Snapper* newspaper reported "A nice hayride in Lancaster County on a Saturday night? To anyone who lives outside the area, they'd think you were on an Amish tour through the fields—to anyone in the Field of Screams, they'd know you're on the most frightening hayride around!" A twenty-five -minute, fright-filled ride through the cornfield takes patrons past scary scenarios only found in their worst nightmares.

There is no turning back as the journey begins into the tall, swaying rows of corn. Pulses rise and hearts pound as the wagon winds further into the field. Customers will first encounter blood-hungry pigs and maniacal farmers in the slaughterhouse. As the barn doors lower, you are trapped in the slaughterhouse of a deranged farmer where the pigs are carnivores. Pig corpses drop above your head and drip blood all over the wagon.

You are released from the slaughterhouse only to find yourself in an even more terrifying situation, The S.H.A.D.E. detention facility. This facility is a cryogenic experimental lab overtaken by mutated creatures. Deafening sirens blare, disorienting you as you travel through the three chambers of the facility. The mad scientist tries to warn you, but unfortunately, it's already too late as the monsters have taken complete control. The lab-created mutants will not hesitate to take you as one of their own.

If you survive this, you can see fluorescent colors around the next turn. You are entering Mountville's Toxic Waste Dump! Watch out for crashing barrels and toxic chemical leaks. There is a crazed Hazmat worker on top of a tower—and he's throwing a barrel straight at you! You feel a mist come over you—is it one of the toxins? Thankfully the wagon continues to move forward and takes you away from the toxic chaos.

Up ahead it looks like the wagon will enter a circus tent façade. You may think to yourself, "what could be wrong with the circus?" But you quickly learn that those hiding here are not your typical silly clowns. As the insane clowns swing around you on trapeze bars and jump at you from all angles, each movement is more menacing than the last. As you make your way through the mayhem, you leave the sinister clown laughter of the pyscho circus in the background and enter again into the dark cornfield.

In the distance you hear begging screams. As the wagon turns the corner you see a massive guillotine. This is where the screams were coming from, as a young woman pleads for help as the executioner taunts her and the witnesses that have just arrived. Suddenly, lights begin to flash and the killer counts down 3… 2… 1…! The razor-sharp blade comes crashing down and all that is left is her lifeless head rolling down the ramp. You have several moments of eerie silence as you anxiously await the next terror. As the fog clears, there is a massive spider feasting on what appears to be a human corpse.

You are entering an overgrown and abandoned greenhouse where the creatures have control. The doors close behind you and you feel little legs crawling all over your skin. A huge snake hurtles toward your face and misses you by a mere inch. As the greenhouse dwellers come creeping down through the ceiling and walls all you can do is hope that someone will hear your cries. Your fear of bugs takes on a whole new meaning.

As the wagon continues onward, you hear bluegrass tunes, and the smell of moonshine fills your nostrils. Here you meet the Rednecks. These crazy hillbillies seem to have no regard for safety as they carelessly toss around shotguns and gasoline. Suddenly, the gas catches fire due to an errant bullet and the entire cornfield seems to explode!

You try to leave the area without getting burned as you travel towards Skip's Chop Shop. Here you see mutilated bodies hanging from giant claws, a crashed school bus, a fire truck, and an abandoned caboose. Goosebumps cover your entire body as you await your fate. Suddenly, the junkyard maniacs are jumping on the wagon left and right. One of the psycho scrappers begins to scale the towering metal fence and just when it looks like he is going to

jump, the fence crashes down violently into the wagon. The tractor quickly pulls away in an effort to get you to safety and approaches a colorful spinning vortex, The Tormented Twister.

As the wagon continues forward, the bright colors and patterns spinning around you throw you into a daze. You have difficulty seeing straight and the whole wagon seems to be spinning. The mirrors on the walls further your disorientation. Finally, the wagon escapes the vortex and brings you to your next fright. Still dizzy, you slowly make out a sign, Letch's Tunnel of Terror.

Body parts line the walls as you pull through the building. Suddenly, the lights go out and you are surrounded in complete darkness. Then you hear them—the chainsaws! Strobe lights come on and you see Letch and his army attacking the wagon. The saws press against your skin and all you can do is scream. Finally the doors open and you are free to escape. At last, you have made it—and survived one of the longest, scariest, most heart-pounding haunted hayrides ever created!

THE DEN OF DARKNESS

"The Den of Darkness equals three stories and twenty-five minutes of grabbing my friend's sweater!" wrote the *York Daily Record*. As the attendant at the door escorts you into the Parlor Room, you will find yourself shrouded in complete darkness. Suddenly, the Denkeeper flies out at you from behind the coat rack. He welcomes you, and since guests are a rare occasion, he ecstatically confines you to the Parlor, so it seems as though there is no escape.

After finally finding an exit, you are coaxed down into the furnace room. The smells of soot and burning flesh fill the room. The cremator bursts out and slams another body into the furnace. Move quickly or you will be his next victim.

As you climb out of the dirty furnace, you find yourself in a greenhouse where the overpowering sound of buzzing flies makes your skin crawl. As the gardener sits eerily on a tree swing, you try unsuccessfully to pass by without making a sound. She flies toward you from the swing and launches herself across the garden.

Fleeing from this maniac, you enter the garage. The mechanic is working on a car that has crashed into the wall. As he mutters senseless words and utter chaos ensues, his frustration erupts, and he chases you with a rusty, blood-soaked wrench. You barely dodge him only to enter a truly disturbing torture chamber.

Human flesh and body parts are sewn together to embellish the walls. You continue to move through the room, and there is a lifeless body of a man on the table and a woman pleads for help from a cage in the corner. In a flash, the Butcher flies out from behind the table and taunts you with the circular saw that he uses to dismember his victims. Terrified, you sprint away and run into a filthy kitchen.

The stench of garbage and stale cigarettes is so overpowering that you think you may be sick. As you try and escape, the cook jumps out from the pantry. He towers over you, and you find yourself cowering in fear. Another victim catches his attention for a moment and allows you the brief chance to escape. Unfortunately, you run directly into another revolting area—the bathroom, where a lifeless body hangs from the rafters, as blood and entrails drain into the tub below.

After lunging for what you hope is the exit, you find that you have joined a dinner party. Unfortunately, you did not have an invitation and the menu is not to your liking—the guests are feasting on a freshly prepared corpse. They want you to stay to use you as a second course, but you manage to outrun them.

You see a beautiful woman offering you a drink in the ballroom and you think your nightmare has become a dream. But look around—everyone is staring at you, and it is impossible to separate reality from illusion. The dancers, servers, and maids repeatedly startle you. A man swinging across the room like a chandelier is perhaps the most shocking feature of this ballroom.

As you sprint up the stairs, you discover the hallway of fears, where beheaded animals line the walls. Will your head be the next one added to this collection? Around the corner is the cryptkeeper's room. Here the Master of the Crypt will force you to your knees to literally crawl into the blazing fireplace. As you slowly make your way on your hands and knees through this narrow passageway, monsters lurking in the dark warn you to "Watch out for the Rats!"

Finally, you reach the end of the darkness, only to find yourself stepping into the morgue! You must try not to become another body for this room as you attempt to edge past the medical examiner. As you escape, you find yourself in yet another dark corridor. You realize that it is a closet as you shove your way through dusty old jackets that haven't been touched in years. While pushing through the racks of old clothes, The Den dwellers love to play games and slice the ankles of unsuspecting guests.

Finally, you seem to be safe. You climb the stairs to the third floor and find that you are entering a doll room. The dolls taunt you, and though they seem sweet at first, as you continue through the room you learn that they are truly menacing. As you hurry down the steps, you stop. You are entering total darkness. A voice beckons you forward. You proceed for what seems like an eternity through endless whispering hallways, twists, and turns in the pitch-black maze. When you finally reach the end, you walk down another set of steps into a room filled with clanging pots and pans.

The Butcher hears you and fires up his chainsaw. He is headed straight towards you! You barely make your way past him and run through a freezer full of frozen, dead bodies and out the door into to cool evening air. You have survived the Den of Darkness and experienced first-hand what has been written on the entrance door since it first opened in 1995—Pay to Get In, Pray to Get Out!

THE FRIGHTMARE ASYLUM

Your entrance into the Applegate Asylum begins with the brain therapy room. The room is lined with televisions, and the deranged doctor is adjusting the levels on the patients' electrotherapy chairs. The Doctor is unhappy that you have interrupted his practice and is prepared to make you endure the same torture as his current patients. You move quickly to escape him when you find yourself witnessing an operation where the maniacal surgeon is performing a lobotomy. He launches himself over the railing in an attempt to drill into your skull, but luckily you duck away and enter the recreation room.

This area is home to the most ill-crazed Applegate residents and is complete chaos. The smell inside this room is rancid, and the patients cough and sneeze relentlessly. You run away in disgust as you feel a spray of mucus coat your face. You next encounter a patient strapped to a chair, and as he attempts to give you a smile, blood pours from his mouth. All that remains behind his swollen, split lips are a few stained and broken teeth. You attempt to help him when suddenly the Dentist, Dr, Phil Macavetes, bursts through the door and rips out the patient's remaining teeth with his well-used rusty dental tools.

The next room is no less startling as another deranged doctor straps his victims to a table while he performs many invasive tests. If the table is empty, beware! As you move forward, you find yourself back in the recreation room. You haven't forgotten your first experience in this area and sprint away. You squeeze past broken automatic doors and find yourself in an empty room. Everything seems normal until you are blinded by the bright fluorescent lights of the decontamination chamber. Disoriented, you stumble up a flight of stairs to the autopsy room. You have never smelled anything as foul as the stench permeating these walls. You hold your breath as the maniacal pathologist attacks you with a blood-soaked scalpel. You don't want to end up like the mangled-up corpses on his tables.

Making your way through a dark hallway, there is complete silence except for a television set. Out of nowhere, a crazy clown comes hurtling towards you and the sensory overload begins. These hobo clowns want you to join their posse. Everywhere you look there seems to be another clown. When it seems like there is no escape from the flashing lights and noise, you see a dark hallway with inflatable walls. You must maneuver your way through the confining walls to get to the other side. The claustrophobia begins to settle in as you frantically make your way to the end, with no idea of what will be happening next.

A set of stairs leads you to the nurses' room, where six-foot-tall nurses overrun the entire area. Strobe lights flash and it is difficult to know who is real. You try and remain calm, but nurses sporadically pop out to torment you and give you your shots. Just when you think you've managed to escape, you stumble upon the checkered psychotherapy room. The entire space is covered in black and white squares, and the strobe lights make it even more disorienting.

While you fight for the exit, the checkered man crashes through the wall and begins chasing you.

You finally choose a door that leads to a staircase full of cockroaches. The hair on the back of your neck stands up and you feel the roaches crawling all over your body. At the top of the staircase, you are greeted by a group of unique residents. These are different than the other patients you have encountered as they are children. You have reached the attic where the youngest inhabitants of the Applegate Asylum dwell. You are very unsettled by these young patients as they beg for you to stay and play their games.

As you continue further into your nightmare you enter the laboratory, which seems like something from another planet. Vines ooze a poisonous serum and mold coats the walls. You tread quietly through the dark until the Doctor attempts to lure you into being his next subject. He chases you down the stairs and through a door, and you find yourself in a room with padded walls where lunatics rev their chainsaws. They almost catch you as you leap for a slight crack in the wall, hoping it may be the door. You have finally made it away from the mayhem of the Frightmare Asylum!

NOCTURNAL WASTELAND

Your journey through the desolate woods begins as you enter an abandoned ice cream truck. An eerie tune plays and the driver welcomes you into the unknown territory of the Wasteland. As you begin your journey through these wicked woods, you quickly realize that no one will hear your screams for help. You climb a ramp into a rickety, old, school bus that dangles high above the hayride path. Your screams awaken the wasteland residents, and they begin to attack.

You continue on the catwalk, but you don't dare to look down. The ramp shakes and you can't help but be afraid of plunging to your death. You make a run for it and are successful in making it safely back to the ground. The trail leads to an abandoned powerplant, and the workers warn you that this area isn't safe as you experience the surge of electricity firsthand. As you leave, you see a shed in the distance.

The woodcarver greets you and you realize that he has gone from chopping wood to chopping up bodies. Will you be next? As you hurry forward, you don't have to travel far to experience your next fright. The gas station is straight ahead. It's very dilapidated and you are unsure of which direction to take. Suddenly, you realize that the lawn mower is leaking gas and there is a welding torch nearby! As the lawn mower catches fire and the station attendant emerges savagely through the gas shack, he holds a gas can to your lip urging to take a sip. You decline his offer as you rush away.

You pass through a rusted gate that reads Deadwood Cemetery. The first thing you see is a massive, towering tree, The Tree of Death. Rotting pumpkin lanterns decorate its branches, and moss-coated gravestones cover the lawn. There is a layer of fog on the ground that makes it difficult to see your feet as you move carefully through the cemetery. Suddenly, a decaying soul launches itself from its grave and lands directly in front of you. Startled, you search for an exit and run through Paquin's Casket Room where some of the souls aren't quite dead.

You find yourself climbing a few steps to enter another abandoned school bus. This time, the sound of children laughing overwhelms you. All you can see are the backs of the children's heads. Which one will terrorize you? Halfway through the bus, a young girl turns her head a full 180 degrees and stares you straight in the face. This is enough to send shivers down your spine as you sprint out of the bus towards the Trapper shed. Here the hunters that inhabit the wasteland aren't interested in small animals—they are looking for the prime game, humans! You avoid the cages and make your way to the Witch Hut.

The witch is brewing up her latest concoction and she thinks you are the secret ingredient. You inch further through the trail to the Swamp. You can't see what's below you, but you know it can't be good. The thick green water reeks of rotting fish. You look up and see that the stench is coming from a gigantic creature caught in the fishing net. As you are distracted by your disgust, the Swamp creatures come flying out of the water towards your face with razor sharp teeth.

You rush to safety, but find yourself in a water treatment plant. This run-down facility is not safe for outsiders. The water is toxic and one splash on your skin is deadly. You must travel over a bridge to leave this area. While doing so, the bridge begins to shake violently causing you to move even more quickly. You cross over just in time before the bridge crashes into the poisonous water. You turn the corner, and you see lightning up ahead.

As you get closer, you realize it's not lightning, it's a tesla coil sending out shocks of electricity. You bolt through the room to avoid getting shocked and find yourself with the most terrifying attacker of all, The Brander. He comes racing at you with a brand that has the initials NW. The glowing, orange brand is getting closer and closer to scorching your skin until the brander is distracted by a distant siren, and you have just enough time to escape. His friends with chainsaws are nearby and hear your screams. They are tired of cutting up raccoons and squirrels, and they are ready for real prey. You are the perfect victim. Fortunately, you find a secret tunnel that brings you back to civilization. You run faster than you ever have and let out a sigh. You have finally escaped the Nocturnal Wasteland.

SUMMARY

Over the last thirty years, Field of Screams has come a long way from a one-wagon hayride operation to what it is today. With four world-class haunted attractions, Field of Screams gives you more heart-pounding thrills and spine-tingling chills than you can handle. Gene and Jim Schopf pride themselves on providing quality family entertainment at a reasonable price. They believe in creating the best scares possible with the highest quality actors and props. The entertainment value from your experience at Field of Screams in unmatched. Both brothers feel that if people are screaming, laughing, and having a good time with their family and friends, then their mission is complete. They look forward to another 30+ years of FEAR!

Authors

This article was written by Christine Eshleman and Sydney Schopf. Christine has worked full-time for Gene and Jim Schopf since January of 2000, but has been heavily involved with Field of

Screams since its second year in 1994. She manages the Information Center during Field of Screams and manages Schopf Bros. Farms throughout the year. Sydney is Jim's daughter and is a college student studying to be an elementary school teacher, just like her father, her paternal grandfather, and paternal great grandmother (who taught in four local, one-room schoolhouses). She has acted at Field of Screams since 2016 and works at Schopf Bros. Farms during the year.

KYLE LAFLAMBOY

Kyle LaFlamboy first stepped into a haunted house as an actor, 25 years ago, when he was only nine years old… I guess you could say he was born to be a haunter… Or someone seriously violated child labor laws. Over the past two and a half decades, he has moved up through the ranks from acting, to building, and eventually managing. While his brother had him working at the haunted house, his father also had him working on construction sites. This background in construction with his father and theatrical production with his brother led him to study architecture in college. After finishing school, he took his passion for design and his experience in the haunt world and dedicated his efforts to the haunt industry. Since then, he has led the way in technical design, creative concept building, leading build crews, setting the bar with guest hospitality, and he even finds a way to get a costume on every night in October and leads the actors by example. His credits include: Statesville Haunted Prison, The Fear at Navy Pier, Zombie Containment at Riot Fest, and HellsGate Haunted House.

He is currently the Production Manager at the Critically Acclaimed HellsGate Haunted House, General Manager of Legacy Adventure Park, and lead designer for Zombie Army Productions.

Although he enjoys his work being featured on the Travel Channel or winning national awards for his efforts, his greatest reward for working in the haunt industry is being able to work closely with his family and friends every day. He's married to his best friend, Audra LaFlamboy, (who he met through Zombie

Army) and father to Ziggy LaFlamboy, who he can't wait to introduce to the family business of haunting one day.

AS A DESIGNER OF HORROR THEATRE OR EXPERIENCES, EXPLAIN YOUR PROCESS.

I have a background in residential architecture and design—so a lot of my conceptual designs revolve around practicality. Make the space practical and easy to work/manage. If you give the actors and managers an easy space to move and work in, it will always enhance their performance. I had a job as an intern in college designing kitchen layouts for custom homes. We would lay the whole kitchen out and pretend we were cooking or doing dishes in the space.

That's the easiest way to compare that process; thinking about how a kitchen layout would work—you wouldn't put a kitchen sink in a far location from a dishwasher. I use that same process when laying out a room to make sure that the actor/manager has all the tools they need in a proximity to make their job as seamless as possible.

WHEN IS THE LAST TIME YOU WERE GENUINELY SCARED BY SOMETHING SOMEONE CREATED?

I've been blessed enough to see the best haunted houses across the country. I've seen the best haunted house scenes created, so I'm sometimes numb to the actual "scare" part of the scene.

But one of the most memorable scares I've ever experienced was at The Beast in Kansas City. My group and I were stuck wandering in a pitch-black labyrinth for what it seemed like ten minutes. After a while, I took over as the leader of the pack. I've been through enough labyrinths in my life to know if you keep your hands on the walls, you can usually find your way around easily. To my surprise, they had created one wall panel that simulated a lightning strike out of nowhere! The sound and light out of nowhere dropped me like a sack of potatoes. My group had a great laugh at my expense. That specific scare will always come to mind. It was such a simple design but still effective to even the most seasoned haunted house visitor.

TELL US ABOUT YOUR CONTRIBUTION TO OUR BOOK. WHAT WAS THE INSPIRATION?

A lot of people can explain their first night working in a haunted house. I have the unique perspective of telling that story from the eyes of a nine-year-old boy. 1998 was my first season at Statesville Haunted Prison, and I can remember that night like it was yesterday.

WHAT DO YOU LOVE ABOUT THE GENRE OF HORROR?

My favorite part of the genre of horror is how it makes the audience relate. In other genres it seems as though you're an outsider looking into another story. When I watch a scary movie or read a scary story, the feeling of being afraid makes me feel like I'm right there with the characters. I always end up putting myself in the shoes of the characters and think what I would do in that situation, that's why I think you hear people yelling at the screen in a scary movie to "RUN." You don't really see that in romantic comedies. It's why I love what we get to do for a living so much. We're not just building sets; we get to build worlds. It's an amazing feeling to watch audience members embrace that feeling.

WHAT ARE SOME OF YOUR INFLUENCES?

I am very lucky to have the most influential person in my life be such an iconic person in the Haunted House Industry. That would be my brother, John LaFlamboy. He is truly larger than life and I've had a front row seat to soak up as much as I can from him.

Also, my father, John LaFlamboy, Sr. He's always taught me to never settle. He's the hardest working person I've ever seen. His grit and determination truly make me feel like I can accomplish anything I put my mind to.

WHAT IS YOUR FAVORITE HALLOWEEN TREAT?

ANYTHING chocolate. I've always had a sweet tooth, but chocolate is my go-to treat!

YOU ARE HOSTING THE PERFECT HALLOWEEN MOVIE MARATHON. WHAT ARE THE FILMS DO YOU CHOOSE AND WHY?

- *Jaws 1*—Greatest Horror Movie of all time in my opinion, literally changed people's everyday activities. Everyone was afraid to swim in open water.

- *Tremors 1* and *2*—Both two of my all-time favorite movies growing up.

- *Chucky 1*—Only movie that I can remember being terrified of as a kid and having actual nightmares. Never trust dolls!

DESCRIBE THE PERFECT HALLOWEEN.

Halloween is a little different for me, being someone who's been working in the industry since a very young age. I don't have a lot of those nostalgic memories of dressing up and trick-or-treating like a lot of people. Halloween for me marks the end of our haunted house season. It's normally a celebration that we made it through another Rocktober.

I love enjoying the time with my friends and family at the haunt celebrating a successful season. There's always a little buzz in the air from the cast members that night, so I always have a good time seeing them get to have a little fun and enjoy our last night of the season. No matter how long I do this job, I still get butterflies hearing that the last group has left the attraction for the night on Halloween. It means I've done my job to the best of my ability that year, and we're off to the races for another season ahead.

FROM SOCCER PRACTICE TO PSYCH WARD

Fall 1998

I was just getting settled into the fourth grade at a new school for the fourth time in four years.

My father was a general contractor, so we moved a lot for his work.

It was tough every year to make new friends while trying to settle into a new school.

This year, however, was a little different; my oldest brother John was back from school. John had recently just graduated from college and was home all summer with a brand-new job! Unlike a lot of the other kids in my grade, my brother didn't come home to get a sales job or start a new career in the corporate world. The guy I wanted to be just like was building his first ever Pro Haunted House. He and a handful of friends from college had graduated with four-year degrees just to come back home to build what most people didn't understand. You see in 1998, Haunted Houses were not as popular as they are now, especially pro haunts. Haunts back then were thought of as fundraiser activities or just another reason to decorate for a holiday. No one in their right mind would spend four years at a university to then push all their chips in to start a Haunted House company. My brother John doesn't fit in that category of people. To say our family didn't believe in his vision was an understatement. Everyone had thought it was a waste of time, a waste of energy, and most importantly, a waste of an education. That was everyone besides me.

I'll never forget the way he would talk about this dream of this haunted house. How passionately he would describe that he wasn't just designing theatre sets anymore, he was "building worlds." Every day he would drive me to and from school, he would describe to me in detail how he was going to create this haunted house as interactive theatre. To take everything he had learned in college and make the first-ever, actor-based haunted attraction in our area. It was so cool to hear him so excited. Sometimes I thought he was talking to me about his dreams the most because I was the only one who would intently listen. Later, through his design I realized he just needed all of my Lego sets to put his dreams into a physical model. I was more than happy to make the sacrifice.

As the summer wound down John and my conversations got shorter. The gleam in his eyes when talking about what his master plan was, started to look different. It was almost showtime. He and his band of misfit college friends were about to find out if all the doubters were right or not. I don't know if he's ever admitted it or not, but that drove him to work harder. Every time our father would scoff at John's "master plan," John would dig in deeper. But for the first time ever, that hole that he was digging was his, and it wasn't just for him, it was for all the people who had followed him to this point, including me. For the first time, he had a responsibility much bigger than just his own future. For months he had been telling everyone what he wanted to do, now it was time to prove what he *could* do.

Opening Night

A night I'll always remember. I left school on a Friday to head to my travel soccer team's practice. Soccer was a way for me to have some sense of grounding. Even though I had moved so many times, I stayed with the same soccer team over the years. I was good enough to make the travel team with a group of kids that would eventually turn into my lifelong friends. The same way John would talk about how theatre was his foundation, soccer was it for me. Soccer was my safe place. But not that day. I remember for the first time that I couldn't wait to leave the field that day. 'Cause that day was Opening Night.My father was picking me up that day and taking me to the haunted house right after practice. We were, of course, running late. I'm sure my dad could recognize I was antsy in the car.

We finally made it to Sigel's Cottonwood Farm, the host property to Statesville Haunted Prison. I knew my way around the property. I had spent the last couple months picking up scrap wood and recycling screws for John and his build crew. My dad took his sweet time getting out of his truck as I grabbed my things and ran to the barn. To my surprise, it was all so different from than the last few months.When I had been in this building before, it was just a few of us. John, his build crew, and a couple of the farm owner's family. But now, it was full of other people that I didn't recognize at all. The place that I had shared the dream about for months didn't feel like the comfortable space it once had. It was the moment that I realized; I didn't really know what a haunted house was at all. There were people in black costumes and makeup and spitting blood all over the place. Actors playing loud music and dancing wild in the corner. Everyone seemed to be smoking cigarettes. I was terrified. I wandered through the mess of clothes and backpacks piled on the ground (there was no budget for hangers at the time) looking for my brother. I remember spotting him and trying to get his attention. His face was white as a ghost, and he seemed to look right though me. At the time I had no idea what that look was— but looking back on it now, I know exactly what the face means. It means it's opening night. It means all your chips are on the table, your ass is on the line for the next few weeks to see if you can afford to eat for the rest of the year. Just as I was second guessing my involvement all together, I can remember hearing the most beautiful laugh taking over the whole room, it was Miss Vicky Strei.

Miss Vicky was what we now call a "haunt mom." She was another dreamer that stuck to this magnet that was John's dream. She was the sweetest woman I've ever met in my life. Anyone who knew her would agree. She was also my bodyguard from my brother and his college friends. She was always looking out for me, always making sure I was ok. And that night, I needed her more than ever. I ran over to where I heard the laugh come from, and she picked me up like the little child I was. You see, everyone else had a panicked look on their face of what the night was about to be. Not Vicky. She knew her role and she played it well. It was up to her to ease the tension and let us all know it was going to be ok. Vicky was not only our haunt mom, but she was also in charge of costumes (everyone wore many different job titles back then). Vicky had me step aside to wait for a costume for a bit. I was the smallest person she'd probably ever had to put in a costume. Finally, after a short while, it was my turn. My position: a maniac. My costume: an extra small adult white pant suit.

I looked ridiculous. After costumes was makeup time, another thing I knew nothing about.

Luckily, one of those scary people that I was shy about when I first walked in the door helped me out. That seemed to be a common theme about the people in that room. They were all like Miss Vicky, all of them more than ready to help me out. Looking back on it now, they all felt the same way as I felt walking into that barn on the first day, an outsider that really didn't fit in. But that was about to change for all of us.

Showtime

There I sat, looking ridiculous in my white pant suit as people shuffled around making last minute changes. The tech team was running into issue after issue, and the production team was trying to plan for issues that they couldn't see coming. But it didn't matter how unprepared we all were. It was showtime. Out of nowhere I heard John yell, "TO THE PIT!" Everyone looked around, confused. We noticed John walking into another room, so we followed, like we all have to this point. Once we all gathered in a larger dark room, the lights went out. All of us strangers were standing in the dark. We could tell something was supposed to happen, but it hadn't. The first of many tech issues that night. Suddenly, load blaring music started about 30 seconds into a song. Everyone in the room stared around looking at each other, wondering what to do. Some people started dancing and moving around. Then we all got it. This was our warmup. Our very first time doing something together as a team, and the last time we'd be together before our first customers.

Dancing was it. It was the spark we all needed to shake it off. The worry, release all our doubt, and leave behind all of the baggage we carried into that room. As the song ended, we all cheered with excitement. Until we heard a voice yelling above us. It was my brother, John. Standing on an old soap box from a previous job, he started his warm-up speech. He started by thanking us all. He thanked us all for showing up, he thanked us all for believing in this dream of his, but above all, he thanked us for our support to get us all to this point. He tried to explain what to expect in the coming hours. But even he didn't know what to expect. Because there was no way of knowing what that opening night would spark into.

Places

After John finished his speech, he yelled "PLACES." Another confused look around the crowd.No one has ever been in this building, let alone know where the specific room they were working for the night was, but I did. Months of listening to John's design plans in the car on the way to school has led me to this moment. I knew exactly where the Maniac Ward Cell #1 was. Water bottle and flashlight in hand I was ready to work, and I eagerly stepped into my scene for the night. You could hear the music starting to play in the rooms around me. But not my room, it sat silent and dark. Tech issue.

I was nervous at first because I was the only person in the room. Did they really leave a nine-year-old alone on the first night? Of course, they didn't, in walked my older sister Sara. Like myself, she was along for the ride for her brother's dream. Sara is four years older than me, but she's always acted older than her age. It was the first comforting moment of my entire day, knowing that she would be there by my side. So there we were, in a haunted house room for the first time, with no sound, no lights, and having no clue on what we were doing.

We could hear our brother John's loud screams through the building, "LETS SEE IT." Over and over the same phrase "LETS SEE IT!" You could tell he was getting closer to us. Sara and I were suddenly not as comfortable as we were before.

As John walked into our scene, he was obviously shocked to find no lights or sound working. He went over his radio yelling incoherently at the tech team to fix the issue. Once he got his answer, he looked up at the both of us and stopped in his tracks. He looked frazzled, strung out, and even a little scared. But when he locked eyes with Sara and I, he gave us a sort of smile. He was relaxed.

He wasn't looking at a group of trained actors or friends of his that were helping him out. He was looking at his two younger siblings. Two children, children that he has helped raise to this point of our lives. He didn't yell "LETS SEE IT!" to us. Cause he knew we wouldn't know how to react to that phrase. Instead, he leaned in real close to the both of us behind our maniac ward cell bars and said, "Have fun, have fun and go crazy." He then reluctantly left us to make sure the rest of his twisted dream was set and ready for the first customers. Sara and I did just what he said, repeatedly, for the rest of the night. We had fun, and we went crazy.

I'll admit, during the show was a complete blur for me. Random people would walk into our scene, Sara and I would act like exactly what we were, crazy kids having fun. I remember the feeling of scaring these random people was contagious. Once we did it the first time, it became second nature. We were hooked. As the night went on, the crowd seemed to slow down. And just like that, the stage manager had come into the room to release us for the night. A whole day of uncertainty suddenly came to an end. We had done it. We just still didn't understand what "it" was.

The Secret Sauce

After the show ended, the cast and crew all headed back to the main room we originally walked into. Missy Vicky's voice was sweetly, but sternly, yelling to put our costumes back where we found them. The room was full of the chatter of everyone explaining what they had just experienced. I remember my father being backstage and him asking me, "how'd it go." I bet you could have seen my smile from across the room. I was hooked. I was in. The room was buzzing. Just a few hours earlier, we were a room full of complete strangers, now it seemed like we've known each other for years.

As I was returning my tattered pant suit to Miss Vicky, I heard John start to begin a speech. We all turned around to listen intently. You could tell he was a different man then the one who gave the first speech of the night. He had conviction in his voice. Before, he was just a kid out of college with a plan. Now he was a man whose plan had worked. Just like the first speech, he started off by thanking us. Again. He thanked us all for showing up, he thanked us all for believing in this dream of his, but above all he thanked us for our support to get us all to this point. He said something at the end of that speech that I'll never forget. I'll never forget it because he says the same thing every year, even 25 years later. "We can design cool story lines, we can build cool things, but if you took away the building and all the scary things, we'd just be weirdos running around a field. It's all of you that makes this place what it is, you guys are the special sauce."

Over the next 23 years I never missed an October in that building. I rose from being an in-house actor, to a front of house queue-line actor, to an assistant manager, to eventually becoming the production manager of the entire show. My rise to the top granted my brother John the opportunity to expand the company to have more attractions. Over the last 25 years, John and I have worked hand-in-hand entertaining over one million terrified customers in the Chicagoland area.

Statesville Haunted Prison has since shut its doors for good. But I'll never forget my first night in that haunted house. I stepped into that building a kid, and I walked out 23 years later a man. I'll never be able to fully explain what that place meant to me.

I'm blessed to work full time in the haunted house industry. I've been able to turn this passion into a career. I'll never take that for granted. This job will never get old, because at the end of the day, I'm just a crazy kid still having fun.

SCOTT TATER LYND

orn and raised in Pataskala, Ohio, outside of Columbus, Scott has been involved in the haunted house industry all his life. Scott has been acting in many haunted attractions and teaching acting classes around the country for years. He is known as 'Tater' to almost every haunter in the industry. Professionally, he is known as the 'fog guy', as he has been a sales representative for Froggy's Fog for over 10 years. Tater has won many awards and accolades for his haunt acting over the years.

AS A DESIGNER OF HORROR THEATRE OR EXPERIENCES, EXPLAIN YOUR PROCESS.

In the character creation process, it is very important to be unique. Observing the various queue-line actors and in-haunt actors in the current haunts, it is important not to wear out the same character; for instance, clowns or escaped mental patients. One of my well-known characters is Granny. There are very few little-old-lady characters, especially played by men.

WHEN IS THE LAST TIME YOU WERE GENUINELY SCARED BY SOMETHING SOMEONE CREATED?

There are two times I have been genuinely scared.

- Raven's Grin Inn in Mt. Carroll, IL. It is a five-story haunt created by Jim Warfield where you go in, are told creepy stories in the dark, threatened to have your finger snipped off with a garden snip, you don't know if you will ever find your way out, and there is no cell service! No actors or fancy props needed here to scare the wits out of you!
- In High School, the movie *Blair Witch Project* had just been released. After viewing the 'found footage,' my friends and I were scared to go back into the apple orchard at night for months!

TELL US ABOUT YOUR CONTRIBUTION TO OUR BOOK. WHAT WAS THE INSPIRATION?

I have been haunting since I was a little boy, this has given me the opportunity to tell my history of haunting and all the things I have had the privilege of participating in.

WHAT DO YOU LOVE ABOUT THE GENRE OF HORROR?

I love the rush of adrenaline after the jump scare, the feeling that you survived and you've 'made it through it'!

WHAT IS SOME OF YOUR FAVORITE HORROR LITERATURE? FAVORITE AUTHOR?

Stephen King, especially his movies

WHAT ARE SOME OF YOUR INFLUENCES?

Kelly Collins (*Terror Park*), Ben Armstrong (*Netherworld*), Allen Hopps (*Dark Hour*), Bob Turner (*Haunted Hydro*), and alcohol!

WHAT IS YOUR FAVORITE HALLOWEEN TREAT?
- Apples!
- Caramel Apples!
- Ludacrisp Apples!
- Evercrisp Apples!
- Goldrush Apples!
- Apples!

YOU ARE HOSTING THE PERFECT HALLOWEEN MOVIE MARATHON. WHAT ARE THE FILMS YOU CHOOSE AND WHY?
- *Cabin in the Woods*—just a bad-ass movie with a twisted ending.
- *Tucker & Dale vs. Evil*—horror and humor done well.
- The Original *SCREAM*—Easter eggs with nods to old horror films

IF YOU COULD CONTINUE ANY HORROR STORY (BOOK OR FILM), WHAT WOULD IT BE?
Tucker & Dale vs. Evil Part 2

DESCRIBE THE PERFECT HALLOWEEN.
Friends and Family gathered for apple picking and Apple Cannon shooting, followed by visiting a local Haunted House at night. Then come back home to a bonfire and games.

HUMOR COLLIDES WITH HORROR

I started in the Halloween "scaring" business with my dad when I was eight years old. Dad was instrumental in starting the Pataskala Haunted Forest with the local Pataskala, OH Lions Club. This year will be the 34th year of the Haunted Forest. Dad would be so proud. Back then, the teenagers were given an area of the trail to design and act. They would have to create their own scene around the theme for the season, using their own props, lights, sounds, costumes, and imagination. Year after year, the areas got bigger and better, and as I got older, I learned more and more from the "Dads" and older kids.

In High School, I joined the Central Ohio Feature Creatures. It was an Acting Troup, led by President Kelly Collins, who owned Terror Park at the time. There were professionals and enthusiasts in the group to get together for prop-making sessions, acting seminars, mold making classes, life castings, and general discussions on all things haunting. Later, in the mid '90s, I went to work with Kelly at Terror Park as a haunt actor, moving my way up to a queue line actor.

I have been traveling around the country for over 20 years as a Haunt Actor. I cannot really count all the haunts I have been to, but they have been on the west and east coast, and everywhere in-between. My two main characters are Granny and Do-Wayne Hazzard.

Folks ask me about my Granny character quite a bit. What was my inspiration for the character? Is she like either of my real Grandmothers? Why an old lady? Are you embarrassed dressing like an old lady? So, to start, when I wanted to come up with a character unique for me, I wanted to be something unique. I wanted the character to fit my body size and style. I wanted something that I would be comfortable with. I am not a large-framed person, so my size could not be intimidating. My human ability is to be a "smart ass," with no screaming at the top of my lungs. Most actors are always 'scary,' so I decided to be 'funny and sarcastic.' I felt as if I needed to diffuse the scare from those that came to the haunt that were truly terrified. I wanted an element of humor, to make them feel at ease. I wanted those people to enjoy themselves, to have fun, to want to like coming to a haunted house. I wanted them to come back! I feel as if there is room for humor in haunted attractions. Being scary is not really in my wheelhouse, so being Granny fit me perfectly.

My Granny character is really not like either of my grandmothers. They were both sweet old ladies, and not quick-witted. I wear an apple pin on my nasty sweater as homage to my family's apple orchard business. My paternal Grandmother's dress is on the Granny prop produced by Ghost Ride Productions in my home.

My Do-Wayne Hazzard character came out of necessity. Granny made a comment and got banned from a haunted house where I was guest acting. I still was contracted for a second night there. So, I raided the costume room and found what I could. That night Do-Wayne (like you can Do-Wayne anytime you want) Hazzard was born.

I have been given a shot at managing as the Actor Manager for four years at the Akron Haunted School and Laboratory. Also, I did a stint for a couple of years as the guy on the Customer Service line at The ScareFactory. I decided I will just stick to being the funny guy in the queue line (well, and maybe selling some fog machines for Froggy's Fog)!

Wanting to share the haunt acting experience that others have shared with me, and that I have gained over the years, I have enjoyed sharing with others too. I have taught numerous seminars at TransWorld, Chicago Frights, HauntCon, ChristmasExpo, and Texas Haunters. I feel as though I bring a unique perspective on haunt acting, as I don't bring the "scare" concept, but the "humor" aspect.

Conventions have a fun side to them too (other than learning)! Midwest Haunters Convention is always a blast, especially the Pre-show Bus Tour, where I have been Bus #2's Bus Captain for over 10 years. It's known as the Party Bus … we didn't have a very fancy name for it, just what it was all about!

Everyone loves a Birthday Party! Starting in 2021, I decided to have a birthday party, called TaterCon. The informal gathering was held in Orlando and open to all. A great group of haunters just eating, drinking, and visiting the parks. TaterCon 2022 was held in Gatlinburg with my haunt friends to experience moonshine, Dollywood, and random crazy fun and games. We stepped it up a notch for TaterCon 2023 on a five-day Cruise to the Bahamas with over 50 awesome haunters. Don't miss the Boat for TaterCon 2024 in May 2024 for seven days of cruise fun with your haunt friends and family!

As much as I have enjoyed it all, I am humbled to have been honored with several awards and "nods":

- Haunted Attractions Association's HAA Presidents Award

- Dent School House Tater Award

- Ghost Ride Productions "Spud" Lifesize Prop (seen at Universal Studios, Hobbs Grove, and other haunts throughout the US)

- 'Missing' Poster outside The Basement Escape Room in LA

RICKY BRIGANTE

icky Brigante was the founder of *Inside the Magic*, a respected leading source of news and information in the themed entertainment industry, covering theme parks, haunted attractions, and immersive experiences worldwide.

After selling *Inside the Magic* in 2018, Ricky channeled his passion for themed entertainment into becoming a designer of immersive experiences.

As Pseudonym Productions, he has helped to create uniquely interactive entertainment, including four Halloween experiences that blurred the lines between reality and fiction while enticing audiences to push boundaries and step outside their comfort zone.

Ricky's work has been featured in *Entertainment Weekly, USA TODAY, Los Angeles Times, Fox News, Huffington Post, Yahoo!, AOL, MSN, Playboy, BoingBoing, Broadway World, NPR, Business Insider, Engadget, Gizmodo, io9, /Film,* and the *Orlando Sentinel.*

WHAT DO YOU LOVE ABOUT THE GENRE OF HORROR?

It gives an opportunity to explore the worst of humanity and learn how to avoid becoming just that. It's also a fantastic release, allowing you to vicariously "experience" the horrible things we all think about from time to time.

WHAT IS SOME OF YOUR FAVORITE HORROR LITERATURE?

I've been an Edgar Allan Poe fan since I was very young, but my favorite horror tales are ones that aren't necessarily "horror" by genre. Books like *A Clockwork Orange* that offer a glimpse at a dystopian time we hope to never inhabit are the ultimate horror stories for me.

WHAT ARE SOME OF YOUR INFLUENCES?

My earliest memories of horror include watching *A Nightmare on Elm Street* and developing a sick sense of humor thanks to the antics of Freddy Krueger at far too young of an age. The music of Rob Zombie has continued that inspired me to always want to walk that razor's edge between horror and comic relief, even if the comedy comes out of the sheer absurdity of over-the-top situations. In recent years, I have immersed myself in the worlds of "extreme" horror events as inspiration as well.

WHAT IS YOUR FAVORITE HALLOWEEN TREAT?

Halloween Oreos, no question about it. I stalk Target every August waiting for that first shipment to arrive.

130

You are hosting the perfect Halloween movie marathon. What are the films you choose and why?

For the classics:
A Nightmare on Elm Street
The Shining
The Exorcist

For the shock:
Hereditary
House of 1,000 Corpses / The Devil's Rejects
A Serbian Film

For the laughs:
Cabin in the Woods
Evil Dead 2
Young Frankenstein

For the family:
Frankenweenie
The Addams Family

If you could continue any horror story, what would it be?

I'd love to discover what a modern-day *Rear Window* would be like, using today's technologies and connection to the world. I feel like there is already so little privacy left that I wonder what a *Black Mirror* style take on the original would be like.

As a designer of horror theatre or experiences, explain your process.

I shut myself in a room alone, either in complete darkness or with a single candle for light. I have my computer for writing and research. I set the mood with meditative dark, droning tones.

I lie down on the floor. Or pace around. I transition from real life into a world where nothing else exists except myself, my thoughts, and my feelings. And I allow myself to find places in my life where I have felt the worst.

Then I write from there. A stream of consciousness of what I am feeling and why I am feeling it. From that, I remove the feelings that I'd never want anyone else to go through and focus on the parts that I can harness into an experience of horror that won't leave people ruined, but still make them think.

Characters and story emerge only after I've identified the darkness that acts as the underbelly of the experience.

Once I write a scattered treatment of how I can have someone else explore those feelings, I begin to hunt for images and music that make me feel the same way.

Through these references, I write a step-by-step walkthrough with detailed descriptions of what guests feel, see, hear, touch, taste, and smell. No detail is too small.

Once that is complete, I step back and give myself some time to escape those dark feelings before working with others to take further passes at the design to make it feel real for everyone involved, not just myself.

It's an iterative process that is sometimes painful to go through, but rewarding in the end.

WHEN IS THE LAST TIME YOU WERE GENUINELY SCARED BY SOMETHING SOMEONE CREATED?

The second time I did the Blackout experience. It left me angry. Utterly angry. At the experience itself. At the actors involved. At other participants. At myself. Anger is an emotion I very rarely feel—and that scared me.

I can't say I "enjoyed" the experience at all. But I do appreciate its ability to get me to scare myself through real, raw emotion. That was powerful.

DESCRIBE THE PERFECT HALLOWEEN.

We have an incredibly successful season of creeping people out with our latest Halloween season immersive experience. Our staff has the reigns of running it, so my wife and I are able to enjoy Halloween night on our own. We come up with some fun costumes for ourselves, prepare a spirited dinner, watch *The Great Pumpkin*, and give a few small scares to hundreds of excited trick-or-treaters who leave our house impressed by our spooky decorations, with full-sized candy bars in-hand.

The classic Halloween is the best Halloween. That's the one from my childhood.

#NOFILTER

The dedication of fans to an interactive experience is unreal, especially at Halloween time.

A couple years ago, we were in the thick of online privacy leaks and Instagram influencer hell, so we asked the question: What happens when social media truly becomes horrifying?

The result was #NOFILTER, the Halloween, time-immersive experience we created at Pseudonym Productions. It was a bizarre mix of an alternate reality game and immersive theater, with online interactions and six live, pop-up events in Orlando, Los Angeles, and New York. Most of it took place in a fake online social network called Connections, definitely not your usual haunt.

While we wove a story centered around a powerful demon hidden in plain sight, the players were the ones who were ultimately in control. The story played out over six consecutive weeks, during which players could choose sides and decide whether to try to save Taylor, the shallow (but endlessly friendly) Insta-star, or to side with Vokorev, the ever-tempting demon, to wreak havoc on all involved.

As Halloween approached, Vokorev seized control of Connections and demanded that her followers reveal themselves with a display of force. Under her "influence," players began dressing like her, worshipping shrines to her at home, and even sharing photos of themselves smeared in fake (we hope?) blood—all to show their loyalty.

Ultimately, she used her newfound online power to give all players access to each other's accounts, including their private conversations and photos. It took a mere few minutes for chaos

#TEAMV
We connect with
Vokorev, Taylor
"Us" ♥

to take over Connections. What started innocently as memes and silly jokes plastered all over each other's accounts as players logged in and posed as each other, quickly turned truly horrible. Anonymized players began posting hateful messages and publicly revealing personal things that had been said under the assumption of privacy on this fictitious social network.

Within a couple hours, the hate spreading was becoming so brutal that we had to shut it down. It was a shocking demonstration of the true horrors of the Internet rapidly unfolding before our eyes. While the characters, story, world, and social network were all fake—the words being exchanged were quite real. And we stopped it just before it had the chance to cross the line between fiction and reality.

Startle scares and clowns with chainsaws can't compete with the horrors of each other. The fast speed at which players went from friendly play to turning hateful toward each other was frightening.

Ultimately, because of the players' actions, Taylor was murdered by Vokorev in a live event, right before attendees' eyes. They circled around her, powerless to stop what they had put in motion. It was a somber, tear-filled happening, after which, players walked silently back to their cars, reeling from the impact of what they had done.

But as Halloween passed, there was still one week of #NOFILTER left to go. And players were determined to redeem themselves.

In literal mourning for a character's passing, we anonymously received at the doorstep of Pseudonym Productions a surprise bouquet of funeral lilies and a cake written with the hashtag #WeConnect, along with Taylor and Vokorev's names.

From that moment forward, players came together under #WeConnect to make good on what had happened, ultimately driving the ending of the 6-week experience with an ethereal appearance of Taylor to forgive them all, including Vokorev. It was the final live event of #NOFILTER and a night of celebration… with cake.

Horror comes in many forms. And the most horrifying of all is when it's real. For those who played and for us as creators, the six weeks of #NOFILTER really happened. And it was powerful for everyone, certainly a Halloween to remember.

DAVE COBB

ave Cobb is a writer, creative director, and designer of immersive experiences that tell stories in physical places: theme parks, rides, attractions, museums, live shows, and events. He has spent nearly three decades combining location, technology, emotion and interactivity to engage and excite audiences in new and unique ways, collaborating with brands and companies like Universal Studios, Warner Bros., Paramount, Lionsgate, Sony Pictures, and Thinkwell Group.

AS A DESIGNER OF HORROR THEATRE OR EXPERIENCES, EXPLAIN YOUR PROCESS.

I think a horror experience benefits most from figuring out early what the most horrific, most impactful, *emotional* horror the guest could or would feel—the "horror moral" of the story, if you will—and design the entire experience backward from that emotion, or at least put it at the beginning of the third act. Land on that at the end—a sense of true emotional dread—and you've succeeded.

WHEN IS THE LAST TIME YOU WERE GENUINELY SCARED BY SOMETHING SOMEONE CREATED?

Easily: Delusion: Lies Within in 2014. All of Jon Braver's work is pretty amazing; even in their weaker years, I always come out with a handful of moments that, through spectacle or story, really wowed me. Lies Within was, in my opinion, the peak of Delusion's powers, and everything worked. It built a sense of unending dread and a heart-stopping conclusion. It took me a long time to shake.

Before that, my answer would have always been The House of Restless Spirits in Santa Monica, which unfortunately had its last haunting in 2014; it wasn't shocking, or jump scares, or anything over-the-top about it that scared me—it was this quiet, slow, deliberate sense of "did-I-just-see-what-I-think-I-saw" around every corner. It felt like a legitimate haunting, one filled with emotion and dread and sadness, but still compels you to LOOK. And keep looking. And keep looking some more even if nothing's happening because… eventually something will, something quiet, and slow, and deliberate, and terrifying.

TELL US ABOUT YOUR CONTRIBUTION TO OUR BOOK. WHAT WAS THE INSPIRATION?

It's a true story of the best Halloween I'll ever have.

WHAT DO YOU LOVE ABOUT THE GENRE OF HORROR?

On one hand, with visceral scares, I enjoy the rush—I love screaming and then laughing, that dopamine and adrenaline jolt. On the other hand, I also love a slow, turning-of-the-screw tension, especially if the release isn't visceral, but rather dread or unease or unspeakable horror.

WHAT IS SOME OF YOUR FAVORITE HORROR LITERATURE? FAVORITE AUTHOR?

Stephen King, of course. And Lovecraft.

WHAT ARE SOME OF YOUR INFLUENCES?

As I kid, I couldn't get enough of *Universal Monsters* and *Hammer Horror*, all a staple of after-school and weekend-afternoon television. Later in my teens, it was the golden age of home video, and my formative horror became high-concept—*Videodrome*, and high-weirdness—*Society*, *The Stuff*, *The Thing*.

WHAT IS YOUR FAVORITE HALLOWEEN TREAT?

Stay the hell away from my Sugar Babies. And from an experience standpoint, I love the silly/spooky haunt experiences as much as the horror-based ones. My two favorite things in all of LA are always the Griffith Park Ghost Train and Boney Island—not scary in the least, but easily my favorite Halloween treats.

YOU ARE HOSTING THE PERFECT HALLOWEEN MOVIE MARATHON. WHAT ARE THE FILMS YOU CHOOSE AND WHY?

I'd start with *Halloween III* because it's a weird tone-setter early in the evening. I'd follow with something like *Society* because it's super fucked-up and weird and gory, yet you can't take your eyes off of it. Next up would be John Carpenter's *The Thing* to continue the gore and dread. Once everyone was nice and freaked out, I'd close the night with the original *Halloween* because that shit STILL scares me. Anyone still awake after that, would get a late-night after-party showing of *The Stuff* for some drunken LULZ.

IF YOU COULD CONTINUE ANY HORROR STORY (BOOK OR FILM), WHAT WOULD IT BE?

Something Wicked This Way Comes by Ray Bradbury. In the book, the Autumn People came every hundred years or so, so I'd love to see a contemporary version of how Mr. Dark would manifest in today's world.

DESCRIBE THE PERFECT HALLOWEEN.

Doing a caravan with friends to all the local suburban haunts we could find, and then home for some horror movies.

An Evening with
Ray Bradbury
RAY BRADBURY
THE HALLOWEEN TREE

SILVER SPUR

TANGIBLE MAGIC: MY HALLOWEEN WITH RAY BRADBURY

Halloween is always fun—but it's rare, however, that Halloween night contains some actual, tangible magic.

On November 2nd, 2007, I was invited to a Halloween dinner party at Club 33, the private restaurant at Disneyland, on the second floor above New Orleans Square. Dinner was, as usual, lovely—I'd been to the Club a few times before over the years, and always had a beautiful meal in an equally beautiful setting. But this time around was different, because there was a guest of honor, none other than the father of *The Halloween Tree* himself, Mr. Ray Bradbury.

Bradbury was a longtime fan of Disneyland, a personal friend of Walt Disney, and an occasional collaborator with Walt Disney Imagineering—most notably on the original concepts for Epcot— so seeing that it was the 35th anniversary of Bradbury's book *The Halloween Tree*, Imagineers Marty Sklar, Tony Baxter and Tim Delaney decided to throw a Halloween party in Bradbury's honor.

Bradbury may have been frail in body, but most certainly not in brain—he was as giddy as an eight-year-old as he regaled us with many of his Disney-related stories, on what he told us was "his favorite holiday of the year." Deep beneath his wheelchair-bound, 87-year-old skin beat the heart of a poet, an enthusiast and lover of life who ensured all of us adoring nerds in the audience that our mutual loves of science fiction, of fantasy, of what the world could indeed be, was indeed okay. He was so full of passion and wanted to get across to all of us in attendance that HE WAS INDEED ONE OF US, and we belonged together in that moment, not as acolytes, but as co-conspirators, as grand collaborators in the humanity of creativity. It was less about his legacy and career as it was a feeling that HE wanted to celebrate how we all tap into the same desires, the same needs, and the same hopes. It was one of those nights where it was hard to tell who was happier to be there—the audience or the man being honored.

As if a six-course meal with one of my literary heroes wasn't enough, another surprise was in store, not only for the audience, but also for Bradbury himself. We all left the restaurant (nerd detail: we walked through the closed park… with all the lights off!) and gathered around a lone oak tree in the darkened town square of Frontierland, stray brown leaves strewn all over the ground. When Bradbury was asked to flip a pumpkin-themed switch nearby, the old tree lit up with strands of tiny, illuminated jack-o-lanterns—thus, he now had his very own permanent Halloween Tree. "I belong here in Disneyland," said Bradbury at the tree's dedication ceremony, "ever since I came here 50 years ago. I'm glad I'm going to be a permanent part of the spirit of Halloween at Disneyland."

Since then, during every autumn at the park, the unassuming tree is given a glimmering makeover, complete with twinkling orange lights, and hand-painted jack-o-lanterns hanging from its branches, and a plaque is installed at the base of the tree commemorating it for all who visit Disneyland during the Halloween holiday celebrations.

As a parting gift, we were all given signed copies of *The Halloween Tree* book. As I left, I picked up one of the stray (fake) "Disney autumn leaves" carefully art-directed on the ground around the actual tree. Mr. Bradbury invited everyone up for one-on-one greetings and photos, so I nervously waited my turn and timidly went up to meet him, asking him to sign the decorative autumn leaf for me.

"I don't really have much to say, except 'thank you,' your books have meant so much to me… I can't believe I'm here," I blurted to him, my hands trembling and my eyes welling up. As frail as

146

he was, he took my hand, surprisingly quite firmly in his, looked me straight in the eyes—his filled with fire, and life, and heart—and he said wistfully and purposefully to me, "well, you are here, and you're wonderful."I wept, and he held my hand firmly until I stopped weeping, giving me a broad, time-weary yet heartfelt smile, and a devilish, knowing twinkle in his eye. It was a lightning bolt to my soul, enveloping everything he'd said during the evening into a warm, gleaming gem deep inside my chest. It made me truly aware of the power of imagination, and the sacred and wonderful connection that all dreamers have. It was magic incarnate, that brief moment, and it changed my life.

I don't think I'll ever have a Halloween quite as perfect.

Postscript: here are some links to a 25-minute video of the entire event (including much of Bradbury's stories, and the lighting of the tree), my photos, and some Disney blog articles about that night:

https://tinyurl.com/DisneylandBradburyVideo
https://tinyurl.com/DisneylandBradburyBlog
https://tinyurl.com/DisneylandBradburyPhotos
https://tinyurl.com/DisneylandBradburyD23
https://tinyurl.com/DisneylandBradburyParks

JESSICA DWYER

essica Dwyer grew up comfortable in a world filled with the macabre of late-night creature features and sci-fi rubber monsters. From a young age she was drawn to the darker side of Universal Horror Movies, Hammer Films, and strange TV series that most five and six-year-olds would be terrified of like *The Night Stalker* and *Dark Shadows*. It continued into a love of science fiction with *Doctor Who, Star Trek, Blakes 7*. It wasn't just TV & movies for Jessica as she dived into a world filled with books by authors like Clive Barker, Edgar Alan Poe, and HP Lovecraft. Comic books were read by the box full as were *Famous Monsters of Filmland, Fangoria*, and *Gorezone*.

Jessica has written for numerous magazines and websites covering the entertainment industry. She has also written fiction and non-fiction published in anthologies. She's recently published her first entry in a trilogy, *Silver and Rubies*. Jessica's also a producer and is working on upcoming film and TV projects. Her online webzine and *YouTube* channel, *Fangirl Magazine* is still going strong as is her radio show/podcast *Fangirl Radio*, which gives the point of view of female fans of horror, sci-fi, and other genres in the world of entertainment.

AS A DESIGNER OF HORROR THEATRE OR EXPERIENCES, EXPLAIN YOUR PROCESS.

When we do our at-home haunt for Halloween, I like doing something that will flow well and utilize the space we have. We've gotten big enough that we're now in the cul-de-sac and no longer just in the garage. When you don't have a lot of space, you figure out ways to make it just look good. With the canopy tent, we realized it looked like a carnival design so we went with a twisted fair booth with a horrifying and gory snack bar. It worked. :)

WHEN IS THE LAST TIME YOU WERE GENUINELY SCARED BY SOMETHING SOMEONE CREATED?

There was a recent Facebook/TikTok video someone did that really got me. Little girl in her room and her dad flips the light switch, and every time he does, you see a figure in the hall. The last time he does it, the thing suddenly runs at the camera, and you see a close-up of the face. Even with no sound, that got me.

TELL US ABOUT YOUR CONTRIBUTION TO OUR BOOK. WHAT WAS THE INSPIRATION?

It was my life and my journey into what horror really means to me and how my love for it has influenced my entire world. It's as personal a story as I can share.

WHAT DO YOU LOVE ABOUT THE GENRE OF HORROR?

Horror can come in so many guises and ways. There's the horror of love, of death, of fear. Horror films and stories can be used to speak about things we won't normally speak of because it's too uncomfortable, but if you disguise it just right using the black, velvet drape of the genre, you can get people to see something they may never have thought of seeing before.

WHAT IS SOME OF YOUR FAVORITE HORROR LITERATURE? FAVORITE AUTHOR?

This is tough. I love Barker, Lovecraft, and we wouldn't have the same sort of stories if Mary Shelley hadn't written what she had. But Poe just has a special place in my heart. His work is beautiful, tragic, oddly funny sometimes, and he never got the recognition he deserved while he was alive.

WHAT ARE SOME OF YOUR INFLUENCES?

Debra Hill was a trail blazer for women in the world of horror. Joss Whedon knows how to write ensemble and snappy dialog better than most. Clive Barker Is a modern master and we don't have many of them left. Dan Curtis changed the face of horror on TV more than once.

WHAT IS YOUR FAVORITE HALLOWEEN TREAT?

Oh … damn this is hard. It seems I'm always digging around for a mini-Kit Kat bar.

YOU ARE HOSTING THE PERFECT HALLOWEEN MOVIE MARATHON. WHAT ARE THE FILMS YOU CHOOSE AND WHY?

Well, *Halloween* would have to be included because it's sort of a rule. *Masque of the Red Death* because Vincent Price needs to be represented and it's a party movie, right? *Fright Night* because it's one of the best vampire movies ever made. And I'll Include Romero's *Dawn of the Dead* because it's one of the best zombie films ever made (and fits that description of how you can use the genre to speak about things that some people get uncomfortable about.)

IF YOU COULD CONTINUE ANY HORROR STORY (BOOK OR FILM), WHAT WOULD IT BE?

This might be cheating, but I would love to have a live action version of the DC Comic *I, Vampire* (comics are books!) There never has been one done and it's one of my favorite horror series. The original run has some of the most beautiful art around and Andrew Bennett is such an amazing character. And bonus, the main villain is a woman named Mary who started out as maiden fair and winds up the Queen of Blood.

DESCRIBE THE PERFECT HALLOWEEN.

Having the haunted garage be up and running before the kids start showing up. No rain and fantastic weather. Having pizza delivered an hour or so in. Wrapping up and getting everything put away without incident and not feeling too exhausted. Curling up with leftover pizza and candy and watching a Joe Bob Briggs marathon until 4am and passing out. Seriously, how can you fault this?

THE TRIBES OF THE MOON

Why I Love the Monsters and
My Fellow Tribe

Why do I love horror films? That's a question you may be asked a lot as a fan of a genre that has been maligned and misunderstood since the beginning of motion pictures. But it isn't just the movies that were treated with strange looks and gasps. We horror fans have been treated with that sort of reaction since we first picked up a copy of *Famous Monsters* or a VHS tape of *Evil Dead*. Our first *Nightmare on Elm Street* t-shirt we dared to wear, or the first time we really went all out for our Halloween costume …we got the stares.

The answer to the question isn't a complex one but at the same time it is. It isn't just the movies or the monsters, even though those are part of it. It's the people and the culture, it's finding the ones who understand you and get it, who've been there. Horror movies are the genre of the outsider, the one who didn't fit, and within those movies we celebrate that.

It isn't just the films, it's the whole package. Going above and beyond with your own personal haunt for Halloween where your decorations have spilled out onto the sidewalk from your porch. You realize you've spent more on Halloween decorations that year than you have on all the other holidays decorations combined for the last five. But that's okay because it's worth it to see the looks on the kids' faces when Freddy Krueger hops out of those bushes. Then there are the books, the video games, the clothes, the prints, the collectibles… it's a lifestyle and it makes up so much of who we are.

But again, you are asking … why do I like horror movies so much?

And for the answer to that question, I'm going to go way back in time to when I was around five or six years old. I grew up in a speck of a town in the Southern part of Illinois. I was a sickly and overweight kid who lived next to a patch of road right out of *Pet Sematary*. You didn't walk near that road, much less ride a bike on it, and it didn't matter because there was really nowhere to go anyway.

It was lonely, and I didn't have friends because I had a family that was pretty insular. Early on, I started watching a lot of TV and that's when it all started. Right around the same time the bullying about my weight started, I discovered *Creature Features* late at night on PBS. This was the first time I would ever see *Dracula* and *Frankenstein*.

Universal's Classic Monster movies were magic. They were like dark, black and white fairy tales that snagged my young brain in a way that nothing else had. Maybe I was too young, but I don't think so. Because it was here that I found my friends. Within the story of *Frankenstein*, the poor lumbering monster who didn't ask for anything that was happening to him, I found a kindred soul. He only wanted to be accepted. He felt like an outsider because he was shunned for the way he looked. If that didn't speak to a kid who was bullied, I don't know what could.

The monsters in the Universal films were all outsiders. Dracula was unlike any others around him, Larry Talbot's Wolfman hated himself and couldn't control what he was, The Creature From The Black Lagoon was the last of his kind, with no one else to understand him. Somehow my younger self realized these "bad guys" were just as much of a weirdo as I was, and I could relate to them.

Pretty soon my elementary school years were filled with reading comic books like *Tomb of Dracula* and lots more things I was way too young for, including old copies of *Dark Shadows* novels. I even did a book report on Barnabas, Quentin, and the Mummy's Curse in fifth grade. None of the other students knew what the heck this was but I think my teacher did, because I got an A.

High School, not surprisingly, was even rougher, and as I got older, I learned about some new films and fiends who would become friends. *Fangoria* become even more a staple along with *Gorezone*. I discovered Clive Barker, Stephen King, and the magic of VHS horror films. It was also during this time I would get called a Satan worshipping b**** and other more colorful and imaginative words because I liked to wear t-shirts with Freddy Krueger on them.

I was a lone fat girl who liked horror movies, going to a high school with less than 200 students. It was in a town where there were literally no African American families or Latino families. One of the nearby towns is now well known for being one of the most racist areas of Southern Illinois. If you didn't fit a certain mold, you weren't going to have a smooth ride through your time. Needless to say, I didn't have a fun time.

I retreated into the books and movies populated by my friends. These stories were my haven away from the reality of what went on at school or at home. I found something beautiful in the *Books of Blood* and how Clive Barker could turn something horrifying into something seductive with just the phrase he used. And while it wasn't the same as having a group of buddies to hang out with, these characters and creatures, stories and strangeness, gave me a haven and helped me learn.

I grew to realize the strange and different weren't something to be feared. I fully believe that these artists, their creations, and those monsters helped me see beyond the near-sighted eyes and limited beliefs of not only some of my family, but the community that I grew up in. These writers, filmmakers, and everyone involved, reveled in the different, they embraced it. I would sit up late listening to Joe Bob Briggs unleash a string of consciousness history of some of the most bizarre films I've ever seen, and it was a lesson that I soaked in like a sponge. He was my teacher of the transgressive, and I would eventually leave my prom early to head home and watch him host a Mummy movie marathon on *Monstervision*.

In 1990 a movie came out that showed everything I had learned and felt about my monsters and friends. I was 15 years old when I came face to face with the Tribes of the Moon. I would wind up driving an hour and a half to see *Nightbreed* on the big screen in the only theater showing it around me. I was transfixed by the story and by creatures that came alive on that screen. Finding ones who will accept you for who you are, for what you are, for what you love, no matter what. Clive Barker had once again showed us what being an outsider was like and that we only needed to find our tribe to no longer be on the outside. That promise of the breed stuck with me as much as the images of the breed themselves.

When I was 16 (before the prom night with Joe Bob and the bandage wrapped shambling Kharis), I had something magical happen. I went to a horror movie convention. Suddenly … I realized I wasn't the only one like me out there. It was amazing. There was Robert Englund, Doug Bradley, Zacherley, and even Uncle Forry. There were people wearing the same sort of shirts I owned. There were people buying trading cards of Jason Voorhees. And there was Clive Barker, in person.

I wasn't alone. I'd found my people, my tribe. I met Tony Timpone, the man I'd seen as a hero on TV defending horror movies against talk show hosts and angry parents alike. I met Clive Barker and was able to tell him how much his work had meant to me. Teenage me was in heaven.

Of course, after the weekend you have to go back to reality (there's a reason it's called con-depression). but things seemed to get better after that. Maybe it was because I'd realized after all that time there were others out there. People I could just start talking to, without preamble, over the cover of a video cassette or an image from the latest Full Moon Entertainment movie. Either way, it seemed to get better.

I'd eventually get out of that small town, and I'd break free from the seemingly eternal mentality that would be present in a lot of the people that lived there. Not all of them of course, but enough that "different" isn't something you want to be.

I moved far away and through that love of horror films I started talking to other fans online. I found friends, a "fanmily" if you will. I started writing and working in this world that I had been searching for so long. I'd eventually start going to horror conventions every year because of this work. At these shows I found my own breed. This group was as colorful and diverse as anything out of Midian. White, black, brown, straight, gay, and all points in between, and all linked by a love of the monsters who understood us when no one else did.

Why do I love horror, you asked? Why do I love seeing the looks on kids' faces when I scare them on Halloween and then they come back through the door of my haunted garage again and again, year after year? Why do I keep collecting movies, books, and things? Here's my answer…

It took me a long time to finally find my place, but when I did, I knew it. We're the strange and unusual. We're the kids that found a friend in Frankenstein. We all dreamed about running away to where the monsters lived. We are all books of blood to be read by those that know our language.

We are the Tribes of the Moon, and you are welcome here just as I was.

EDDIE MCLAURIN

hile in Chicago at a convention for haunt operators, Eddie ran into a couple and was surprised to discover that they "Do Halloween" as a profession. Like any artist/storyteller, the concept of doing what you love for a living grabbed Eddie. He became determined that Woods of Terror would become his profession. Also, like a true artist, Eddie pumps all of his money back into the attraction. Even though 30,000 people or more will walk through the gates this year, paying ticket prices as high as $17 (worth every penny), Eddie still lives in the house where his grandparents lived on the original property left to him by Father McMillin. Woods of Terror is a labor of love, and that shows in everything Eddie does.

AS A DESIGNER OF HORROR THEATRE OR EXPERIENCES, EXPLAIN YOUR PROCESS.

As a designer of the Woods of Terror, most of my influences come from horror movies, going to haunting conventions (example: Midwest Haunter's Convention), where we would do bus tours. Most of it comes from my own imagination and what I would like to create. Sometimes watching my own show at night shows me what works and what does not work for the next season. A lot of the things I do, I have thought about two to three seasons in advance. I will draw pictures and get blueprints created before I start.

WHEN IS THE LAST TIME YOU WERE GENUINELY SCARED BY SOMETHING SOMEONE CREATED?

Two things that stick out were about ten years ago, I had to lie on this long, sliding board that was laying on the ground, and sliding through the pitch darkness was scary because I thought something was going to hit me in the face. The last movie that I thought was scary on the demon side was *Insidious*, it seems as if it could be true.

TELL US ABOUT YOUR CONTRIBUTION TO OUR BOOK. WHAT WAS THE INSPIRATION?

My grandparents and growing up on our farm. Also wanting to keep the farm in my family. I created this back-story for Woods of Terror with a lot of real people and real facts.

160

WHAT DO YOU LOVE ABOUT THE GENRE OF HORROR?

What I love about the horror genre is the entertainment value. The way you can go to the movies with your friends and family and have a good time and be scared. It is an adrenaline rush and a natural high without drugs. The entertainment value of it has been very useful and helpful to the Woods of Terror as thousands line up each year to see what we have to offer.

WHAT IS SOME OF YOUR FAVORITE HORROR LITERATURE? FAVORITE AUTHOR?

Stephen King would be my favorite author. He has some amazing books that include: *Cujo, Christine, IT, Firestarter, Misery, The Shining, Pet Sematary,* and *Carrie.*

WHAT ARE SOME OF YOUR INFLUENCES?

When I was younger, movies like *Jaws, Poltergeist, Pet Sematary, The Thing,* and *Fright Night* had a big part in influencing me. As I got older and got into haunting with the Woods of Terror, I would travel on the weekends when I wasn't open to see other haunts. NetherWorld, Headless Horseman, The Bates Motel, Niles Haunted House, and more had a big part influencing me at the Woods of Terror. It was not only the haunted houses, it was the people that ran them and how they conducted themselves professionally and ran their haunted house like a business.

WHAT IS YOUR FAVORITE HALLOWEEN TREAT?

Reese's Cups

YOU ARE HOSTING THE PERFECT HALLOWEEN MOVIE MARATHON. WHAT ARE THE FILMS YOU CHOOSE AND WHY?

Poltergeist, The Thing, Fright Night, and *The Lost Boys.*

These are the movies I would watch because these are the ones that made the biggest impact on me. I was at the age where my parents were not monitoring what I watched, and I would stay up all night watching these movies.

IF YOU COULD CONTINUE ANY HORROR STORY (BOOK OR FILM), WHAT WOULD IT BE?
Poltergeist

DESCRIBE THE PERFECT HALLOWEEN.
25 nights of Woods of Terror, doing my highest numbers each night, and watching and enjoying my customers being scared to death. This would put me on the path to paying all my bills and having some profit at the end of the season. Of course, I would be giving all my actors and staff goodie bags and candy.

HISTORY OF THE WOODS OF TERROR

I n 1941, during the Great Depression, many people perished from the tolls of hard times. Poverty, hunger, and anger at the world fueled emotions. Those who perished during these times were often not given a proper burial due to the lack of money. As were their bodies not laid to rest, neither were their spirits. These spirits haunted their old homes, places of employment, and city streets with an endless amount of anger. Many cities dealt with this in different ways, some just suffering through the day-to-day agony of things stolen by spirits, not sleeping during the night because of the insistent pacing of hallways and stairs, and the fear of how far the spirits would go to remove the living from the homes they used to own. The city of Greensboro would have had to suffer through these day-to-day agonies if it weren't for a local priest. This local priest exercised and bound these spirits to a plot of land twelve miles from the city limits. This local priest, not knowing where to keep these spirits to where they could not harm anyone, bound them to a plot of land that he himself owned, on the outskirts of town. This priest was Eddie Howie McMillan, the great, grandfather to Eddie Howie McLaurin.

In 1970, Father McMillan passed away and deeded this land to his great, great grandson Eddie H. McLaurin, who was only four months in his mother's womb. As you would guess, for twenty years, these spirits stayed bound to this patch of land. Over his childhood and early adult years, Eddie learned what his grandfather had done, and what exactly inhabited the woods. As time passed, Eddie learned the true power of the spirits and how important it was to keep them imprisoned here. Eddie also learned how to handle and control these spirits through the Holy Spirit, which came upon him after accepting Christ as his Savior at the age of thirteen. He could not control these spirits alone, only through Jesus, who controls all things. Not only did he learn to handle and control the existing spirits, but he also learned how to capture other spirits that are not among the living and not among the dead and release them into the same plot of land that his grandfather before him did. This plot of land is known as Purgatory to the spirits, and to humans, it is Woods of Terror.

It wasn't long before Eddie knew that this land was useless and the taxes on the land were outrageously expensive. The thought came into mind to use the land as a salvage yard where people could dump the old junk they didn't need anymore, and while Eddie charged for the dumping, he could cover the cost of the taxes on the land. A lot of different people brought a lot of different stuff out to the Woods of Terror that was useless to them and that they couldn't use anymore. As the years went on, the spirits of Woods of Terror began to move, rearrange, and construct this junk into scenes that made them feel at home, and naturally, makes you feel uncomfortable…

MIKE SCHWALM

Mike Schwalm is an expert at translating inspiration and stories into striking images. Previously a creative designer for Disney Imagineering, Mike is currently the lead concept designer at Mousetrappe. He provides concept images, storyboards, and art direction for projects ranging from Disney castle spectaculars to cultural installations. Relying on his skills in set design and illustration, Mike creates both beautiful concept images and detailed design packets. His work at Mousetrappe has included concepts and storyboards for the new Disney nighttime spectacular, Happily Ever After, as well as model studies and art direction for the Enzo Ferrari pre-show at PortAventura's Ferrari Land.

During his five years at Disney Imagineering, Mike was involved in concept development for experiences based on some of Disney's most popular IPs. He worked with Lucasfilm on concept development for an Indiana Jones-themed bar in the new Disney Springs shopping district, and also spent three years working with filmmaker James Cameron to bring the immersive world of Avatar to life in Disney's Animal Kingdom.

Prior to working at Disney, Mike did freelance concept design and illustration work with Victory Hill Exhibitions, designing interactive exhibits for both the Avengers and Transformer properties. During graduate school Mike illustrated children's books for Jackson Fish Company.

AS A DESIGNER OF HORROR THEATRE OR EXPERIENCES, EXPLAIN YOUR PROCESS.

Think of something cool. Then make it in a very slow painstaking process over the months before Halloween. Five minutes at a time. Between, work, going to the grocery store, putting the baby down for a nap, getting the baby up, cleaning up the kitchen, infinity trips to Home Depot to get stuff, putting the baby to bed, date night, gym, work, drive, date night, sleep, baby, store, nap, Home Depot, work, sleep, baby, wife, Home Depot, scotch…. Then stand in wonder on Halloween and marvel at how anything ever gets done.

WHEN IS THE LAST TIME YOU WERE GENUINELY SCARED BY SOMETHING SOMEONE CREATED?

The Delusion show in LA. 2016. It was called His Crimson Queen. Best Haunt I've ever been to. At the end I got separated from my group and taken by a Vampire Bride and locked in a coffin. Everyone else had to come rescue me. Terrifying.

TELL US ABOUT YOUR CONTRIBUTION TO OUR BOOK. WHAT WAS THE INSPIRATION?

My first big haunt. *Jurassic Park* was the inspiration.

WHAT DO YOU LOVE ABOUT THE GENRE OF HORROR?

Hiding behind pillows on my couch in the dark, clutching a rosary to keep me safe from the demons on the TV.

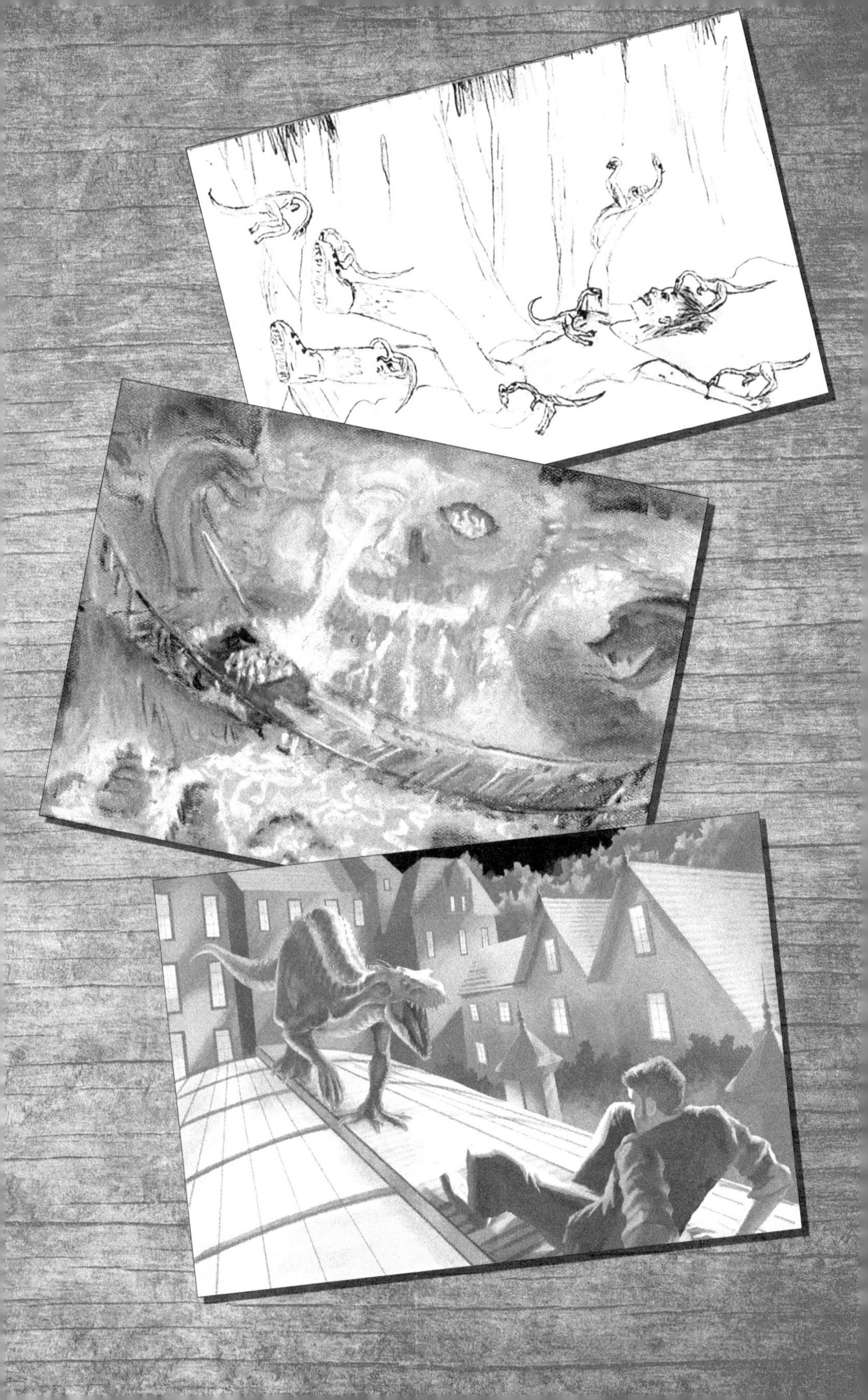

WHAT IS SOME OF YOUR FAVORITE HORROR LITERATURE?
Does that involve reading books?

WHAT ARE SOME OF YOUR INFLUENCES?
Jurassic Park, *The Mummy*, *Indiana Jones*, also *The THING*. The John Carpenter one. Not the CG trash that came out recently. Can I say that? The *Insidious* Franchise. Also, *Jurassic Park*.

WHAT IS YOUR FAVORITE HALLOWEEN TREAT?
Scotch.

YOU ARE HOSTING THE PERFECT HALLOWEEN MOVIE MARATHON. WHAT ARE THE FILMS YOU CHOOSE AND WHY?
I like the creature features so, *Aliens*, *The THING*, *Pumpkinhead*, and *Jurassic Park*.
Or the *Insidious* movies. They are haunted house movies done well. If you scare the crap out of me without getting too violent or gory, you win.

IF YOU COULD CONTINUE ANY HORROR STORY, WHAT WOULD IT BE?
I would keep the *Insidious* storyline going.

DESCRIBE THE PERFECT HALLOWEEN.
Hiding within my garage creation, drinking scotch, and jumping out at children.

LOST WORLD

I've wanted to design theme parks since I was as small as I can remember. My first memories are of Disneyland, and I spent most of my childhood building models of theme park rides out of construction paper or Legos. Any time I would see a new movie, I would race home and design the theme park ride version. I would draw a map of the attraction first. Followed by storyboards and a model.

When *Jurassic Park* came out, it became my obsession. I had every action figure they made and would spend all of my free time playing with them. I built various versions of *Jurassic Park* rides to the scale of my action figures in my back yard. Jeep rides, flying rides and yes, even a boat ride. The boat ride was built by propping a large panel of wood onto a table and covering the ground, board, and table with the blue, Slip and Slide tarp. The blue tarp, of course, became the water, sand from our sandbox and small branches torn off of bushes were arranged to create the banks where the Dino exhibits were. Popsicle sticks and string became the electric fences, while cardboard boxes became facility buildings. Plastic bathtub boats with *Jurassic Park* stickers on them served as the ride vehicles. The boats, filled with action figures, would move through the tranquil Dino exhibits on the ground before traveling up the wooden panel onto the table. It was here where the mean dinos would escape and menace the boat before it plunged back down the wooden board. This was all before I knew anything of Jurassic Park: the Ride.

My obsession didn't stop there. After *The Lost World* came out,

I asked the manager of the Air Force base country club if I could be in charge of their annual haunted house. I had an idea for a Lost World-themed walkthrough I wanted to build. Keep in mind I was 13. Anyway, he had faith in me, and I spent the rest of that summer and half the fall, building giant dinosaur puppets, bones, and cages. My mom and I enlisted many of our family friends to teach me how to build, as well as how to manage sound, lighting, and all those other things I hadn't thought of before volunteering to do this. The local newspaper got wind of the thing and sent a reporter to write a little article about me.

Future Imagineer Trains
on Halloween Fright

Thirteen-year-old Mike Schwalm's dinosaur-themed haunted house is only the beginning. He says he wants to make designing amusement parks his career.

By Jan Jonas
Tribune Reporter

How do you make a dinosaur drool? No, not how do you make a dinosaur drool, but how do you make it look as if one is drooling? Dribble hot glue down its face.

Any good "imagineer" would know that, and Mike Schwalm, 13, wants to be a good one. Imagineering is the name Disney has given to the process of designing its amusement parks, and imagineers are the people who do it.

And that's just what mike wants to do, though he isn't content to wait until he's "old enough." He's plenty old enough now.

One of Mike's latest ventures is his Jurassic Park inspired haunted house, which opened Sunday at the Coronado Club on Kirtland Air Force Base.

Here, a life size dinosaur rib cage is fashioned out of insulation pipe painted white. Cardboard toilet

paper rolls make up dinosaur claws. Raptor cages come from large cardboard boxes and spray paint. And dinosaur bones are carved out of Styrofoam with an electric carving knife—with Mike's mom's permission.

A Tyrannosaurus Rex's skin feels real. Layers of newspaper covered in Phlexglue create the right effect for touching -if you just can't resist.

About 30 volunteers play the part of tour guides, dreamers, and dinosaur snacks.

Mike had been working on the project since last summer when he received permission from the manager of the Coronado Club to set it up in the private club's basement.

But if you think the basement is the only place filled with Mike's imagineering handiwork, take a look at his house.

The patio at his Northeast Heights house, which he shares with his mother, Connie Schwalm, is littered with chicken wire, cardboard and paint dribbled buckets.

"I wonder if we need a treatment for this obsession," Connie says.

Mike blushes, then says, "I always knew I wanted to build stuff, I learned about imagineering, and I completely flipped out. This is what I want to do."

Mike, the youngest of four children, has designed amusement parks since he was a kid, he says. That would be before his latest project to set up a haunted house based on Jurassic Park and The Lost World, two of his favorite movies.

Steven Spielberg is his hero. The Indiana Jones movies are the best, He says.

"I've been on the Indiana Jones ride at Disneyland about 40 times," he says. As he describes it, his blue eyes dart around the room. He flails his arms in rhythm to a beat only he hears as he talks about the scary parts of the ride.

Mike's favorite video is one taped from the Discovery Channel on how amusement parks are built. He watches it often while creating disgusting things for his haunted house.

The home schooler also gets ideas from summer amusement park "pilgrimages" with his mother.

He's been to two Six Flags parks in Texas, Six Flags Mid-America, Disneyland and Disney World, Busch Gardens and Kings Dominion in Virginia, and Universal Studios in California.

The best amusement parks? Mike picks Disneyland and Disney World

This summer will include trips to Ohio and Virginia for the thrill of the ride. No, not the one in the car.

I think people enjoyed the haunted house even knowing that most of it was built by a 13-year-old. Parts of it really were scary, mostly thanks to dark, and fog, and loud noises. I learned so much from the whole experience and it further fueled my drive to design theme parks.

I have worked in the industry now for eight years along with many of my childhood heroes on some dream projects, but that dream JP project continues to elude me. My inner 13-year-old hopes beyond hope that that project comes soon.

ED TEREBUS

dward Terebus Worked as a Locksmith and went to school for fine arts. Joined his brother James doing their first haunted attraction in 1981. Turned the Haunted Attraction business into a full-time career in 1998, when they bought the building now known as Erebus. Erebus Haunted Attraction held the Guinness Book of World Record for the longest walk-through haunted attraction. 2005 – 2009. They were the first to bring that record into the USA. James and Edward, along with their team, have been instrumental in many of the advancements within the Haunted Attraction Community. Produced the *Fear Finder Halloween Tour Guide* since 1993. The paper, 40 pages and 600,000 copies, features all the haunted attractions in southeast Michigan.

AS A DESIGNER OF HORROR THEATRE OR EXPERIENCES, EXPLAIN YOUR PROCESS.

It all starts off with selecting a theme. From there, we orchestrate what kind of scares will happen, from small to large, and what kind of reactions we can expect to see out of those scares. What directions will they be looking at and moving while reacting? This is what allows us to keep everyone entertained and also moving forward. Lastly, the focus turns to the more creative aspects, decoration, lighting, sound and reset value.

WHEN IS THE LAST TIME YOU WERE GENUINELY SCARED BY SOMETHING SOMEONE CREATED?

Unfortunately, being in the haunted attraction business for 40 years has toughened my ability to be scared. So, it has been a long time since I've been scared from something someone else created.

There was this one time many years ago, we had a show no mercy policy. If somebody was scared, get them good! I would even set people up, I would scream out, "don't scare them" and that was the actors cue to come out and scare the yell out of them. This one time, there was a bigger woman passed out, laying on the floor. I was the first guy onsite, and I thought maybe she was having a heart attack. Immediately, I had someone call for help. The woman came to, and I immediately yelled out don't scare her, not thinking about what I was saying, but I really meant, don't scare her! The woman refused to go back to the nearest fire exit because she had to pass what scared her. So as we move forward, the actors jumped out and scared the heck out of her. She passed out four more times in the haunted house. As we got her outside, she'd walk five feet and pass out. Because she was a woman, we could not hold her up, we just had to prevent her from hitting her head. She then jumped in her car and was going to drive away. I reached in from the passenger side window to grab her car keys, thinking she was going to pass out and crash her car. This woman grabs my arm like a chicken leg and took a big bite out of me! I was screaming and she was screaming as the fire department pulled up. The EMS workers kept me longer than her because a human bite wound is very infectious!

Tell us about your contribution to our book. What was the inspiration?

Many people think we just moved into this massive, haunted house, when in actuality we came from very humble beginnings. I would like to let people know that our first haunted attraction was very small, and we grew little by little, year to year, from there. To share the story of our growth over the last 40 years and to look back and appreciate what it took to get here.

What do you love about the genre of horror?

Halloween is hands down, my favorite holiday, as you may have guessed. Not that I don't love the others, but Halloween carries this rare air of no judgement. The Halloween season allows us to become something outside of ourselves, be it scary, goofy, funny, or just plain different. And for whatever reason, people are open and accepting of it. That is what ignites my joy and passion for Halloween and the reason I've dedicated my life to it.

What is some of your favorite horror literature?

No particular author comes to mind, but we did find our latest haunt's name while thumbing through a vampire novel. The word "Erebus" came up and caught my eye because "Terebus" is our last name. After looking up what Erebus is, we knew we had exactly the name we were looking for and felt that we were born to do this!

WHAT ARE SOME OF YOUR INFLUENCES?

We live, eat, sleep, and breathe haunted houses every day of the year. Not sure it has much to do with influence, but more in the way of how we see things, our perspective of the day to day that people don't see through our eyes. The loud barking dogs that the neighbors had or the two guard dogs at the storage lot transformed into vicious undead dogs of the cemetery. Or a puddle up against a building in the middle of a parking lot after a rainstorm, giving us motivation for one of our greatest displays, the bottomless pit. Lastly, speaking with likeminded individuals at the trade shows and sharing in the experiences and laughs over the years that might spark a new idea!

WHAT IS YOUR FAVORITE HALLOWEEN TREAT?

I know it is kind of a hate it or love it candy, but candy corn, and I love it!

YOU ARE HOSTING THE PERFECT HALLOWEEN MOVIE MARATHON. WHAT ARE THE FILMS YOU CHOOSE AND WHY?

Alien and *Aliens.* These two movies were suspenseful and scary from start to finish. And the beauty is that those two emotions stemmed from never knowing where the monsters were coming from or what was going to happen next!

DESCRIBE THE PERFECT HALLOWEEN.

My family getting dressed up in our costumes. Sloppy joe's and chili on the stove filling the house with that unmistakable smell. Taking the kids out for trick-or-treating on a cool evening with Halloween music in the air from all the homes passing out Halloween goodies. The laughter and excitement on my children's faces. Returning home and then jumping into the car to drive to the haunt while my brother's holding down the fort. Approaching the haunted attraction, seeing searchlight sky for the entirety of the drive and finally, arrive to the line of excited people wrapped around the building.

EREBUS
WWW.HAUNTEDPONTIAC.COM

GUINNESS
WORLD RECORDS

CERTIFICATE

The longest walk-through
in a horror house is
667 m (2,189 ft)
at the Erebus Haunted Attraction
in Pontiac, Michigan, USA

GUINNESS WORLD RECORDS LTD

THE HAUNTED HISTORY OF EREBUS

In the late 1970s, my brother Jim worked with one of the local JC chapters doing their haunted house. In the year 1980, my brother was laid off from Ford Motor Company. After the lay-off he decided to build his own haunted attraction. He was 28 and I was just graduating high school at the age of 18. Our first haunted attraction was 1200 square-feet. It was a freestanding building set up in front of a local Kmart. We had all the exterior walls up on the first day, but with one little problem, no internal supports. That evening, 60 mile an hour winds came through and wiped out the whole building. We spent three days reconstructing and setting up the rest of the attraction. Not to mention, we set up on the lower part of the parking lot, so every time it rained, the patrons walked through three inches of water. All part of the ambience that year! That first year we charged $1.50 for admission. We lost $500 when all was said and done.

We decided we needed to approach this in a different way. Jim found some mobile home trailers that were 12 feet wide by approximately 50 feet long that had been damaged by flash fires. We spent all summer stripping, repairing, building, and decorating these trailers for the following Halloween season. That year we charged $3 and the haunted house consisted of 2800 square feet. The following year we added a fifth trailer in the center of the castle to increase the space to 3500 square feet. We ran that unit for 13 years. We donated those trailers for a dollar to a church that ran a haunted attraction. We acquired ten mobile offices that were 14 feet wide by 70 feet long, approximately 9,800 square feet. We ran that unit for seven years. While running this unit and looking at the cost of storage, transport, permits, temporary electricity, temporary water, lot rental, set up time, available operating time and teardown time, we decided to look for a permanent structure.

In 1998, we purchased a building with 113,000 square feet. I sold my house, and my brother remortgaged his because no bank was going to give us a loan for a haunted attraction. Living in that building, I went eight years with no paycheck, just so we could pay off the loans. Working on the attraction, still debating on what we should call it. We're looking for a single word, something like what Madonna represents in the music community. I was reading a vampire novel and it started talking about Erebus. I was not familiar with that and intrigued my interest, because if you put a letter T in front of it, that is our last name, Terebus. Erebus, by Webster's definition, is the darkness beneath the earth that the dead must pass through to reach Hades. In Greek mythology, Erebus is the brother of night and son of Chaos. Perfect!

We opened in the year 2000. In the year 2005, we took the Guinness Book of World Record away from a haunted house in Japan for the world's largest walk-through haunted attraction. We held that record for five seasons until 2009. The record was 2,189 linear feet. We are now over 2600 linear feet, that's the equivalent of walking the length of over seven football fields.

Michigan has always been very popular for haunted attractions. At one point we had over 100 attractions within a 50-mile radius of us. Because of that fact, we couldn't go to the trade shows and buy the really cool stuff because everybody else would have the same thing. It forced us to be more innovative and create things here at Erebus that you can't see any place else. Many years ago, we tried having the actors touch people. We soon found out that was not a good idea, so we created things that would grab you, bite you, land on top you, and we will even bury you alive, how long can you hold your breath? Haunted attractions are a tradition, a rite of passage once you finish trick-or-treating. That is what keeps the Halloween spirit running forever in our young souls!

EREBUS
STORY
EREBUS

HAUNTED GALLERY

Erebus Definition:

According to Webster's dictionary Erebus is the darkness beneath the Earth that the dead must pass through to reach Hades.

In Greek mythology Erebus is the son of Chaos and the brother of Nye (Night).

According to Ron Leadbetter in *Encyclopedia Mythica*: Erebus was known as the embodiment of primordial darkness, the son of Chaos (who was the void from which all things developed, known also as Darkness). According to Hesiod's *Theogony*, Erebus was born with Nyx (Night), and was the father of Aether (the bright upper atmosphere) and Hemera (Day). Charon, the ferryman who took the dead over the rivers of the infernal region, is also said to be the son of Erebus and Nyx.

Later legend describes Erebus as the Infernal Region below the earth. In this version, Hades was split into two regions: Erebus, which the dead have to pass through shortly after they have died, and Tartarus, the deepest region, where the Titans were imprisoned. Aristophanes' *Birds* says that Erebus and Nyx were also the parents of Eros, the god of Love.

He is often used metaphorically for Hades itself.

The Name:

The owner's last name is Terebus, remove the "T" and you get Erebus.

Story:

Erebus is the result of Dr. Colber who worked for the government to build a time machine. After being fired and stripped of his certifications, he began work on the time machine on his own. Eventually he was successful at sending people back into time, with only one glitch. The destination time-period looked at the people as a virus and wiped them out. Determined to overcome this glitch, he sent in group after group of his own personnel. Ultimately unsuccessful, he ended up broke and lacking the proper personnel to run his machine. It is then that Dr. Colber came up with a brilliant idea, to disguise his time machine as a haunted house and have the general public help fund his project and use the people going through as his human guinea pigs.

Stats:

Erebus is four stories high!
- A walkthrough, the attraction is the equivalent of covering a distance of seven football fields!
- Erebus has 125 employees, 90+ of them actors, who work every night during the open season.
- In the off-season, six of them work part time while another five of them work full time all year long. (Many of Erebus' one-of-a-kind props are built in the off-season)
- Most of the props in Erebus are one of a kind.

"It's almost like a Broadway performance; the day after it closes for the season, we are in there working on it full-time for the next year."
— ED TEREBUS, OWNER

A Haunting History:

Erebus was founded in 2000 by Ed and Jim Terebus, 40-year veterans of the Haunt Industry.
- Erebus has gained national recognition as being one of the top haunts as well as being placed in the *Guinness Book of World Records*.
- Erebus leads its Patrons through four stories of unique and terrifying paths with fear so intense some call it pain!

Haunting Facts:
- Erebus is Four Stories, three levels above ground and one underground.
- Over a half-mile walk inside the building.
- The owners' have over 80 years combined experience scaring people.
- Erebus is very interactive; there are sections where things will bite you, fall on you, touch you, jump out at you and scare you in ways you never imagined possible.

- Erebus appeals to all five senses: the smell of chainsaw gas or dry, creepy air; the touch of textured walls; the sounds of screams and laughter; the taste of fear creeping all around you; and the sight of some of the most mutilated monsters and scenes you'll ever see.
- Erebus Haunted Attraction held the Guinness Book of World Record for the longest walk-through haunted attraction from 2005 – 2009.
- 90% of all our props are built by Erebus, guaranteeing our show will be unique and different than any other haunt in the world.
- Over 450 people chicken out and 56 people pee themselves per year…
- (confirmed by managers).
- Since the beginning of Erebus, we've had 8,617 people chicken out and exit before the end and 1,074 people have peed themselves.
- Beaumont Doctors did a study here on fear and concluded that going through Erebus was like an aerobic workout for your heart.
- Looking to have some fun without fear! Check out Erebus Escape—Our Premium Escape Room Destination! Located just 6 blocks north of Erebus Haunted Attraction in Downtown Pontiac, MI. erebusescape.com #funwithoutfear

MATTHEW SANDERSON

Mathew Sanderson is a freelance author who has been writing for horror roleplaying games since 2012. To date, he has worked on more than 20 books for popular game lines including *Call of Cthulhu*, *Kult: Divinity Lost*, *Vampire the Masquerade,* and *Fear Itself* among others. He can often be found at UK gaming conventions, running games to scare his players to the best of his abilities. Matthew lives in the UK with his loving wife, Tiffany, and a growing flock of adorable birds and chickens.

AS A DESIGNER OF HORROR THEATRE OR EXPERIENCES, EXPLAIN YOUR PROCESS.

In my opinion, there are several core elements that can form the foundation of a tabletop horror roleplaying game scenario: an antagonist (e.g. a monster, a manic killer, an evil cultist, etc.); the setting (being a combination of the physical location as well as the time period); or something that has otherwise inspired the author, such as an event (e.g. a murder), or an item (e.g. a cursed doll), etc.

When one of these elements appeals to me strongly enough that I feel a story can be crafted around it, I start to think about how it could relate to the other core elements. For example, it makes sense for a scenario pitting the players against sea monsters to take place somewhere near or on the ocean, rather than in the middle of a desert.

The rest of the story grows organically from there. The important thing about writing a scenario is to keep in mind that the players should be the stars of the story. It's my job as the writer to present as many opportunities as possible to unnerve, scare, and terrify them from the start all the way to whatever climax they may reach. That's what makes it a "horror" game after all!

WHEN IS THE LAST TIME YOU WERE GENUINELY SCARED BY SOMETHING SOMEONE CREATED?

Honestly, I scare easily! That said, I detest jump scares. I much prefer spooky imagery and atmosphere above cheap shocks. The last time I think I experienced a genuine scare was when I went to watch *The Lady in Black* at the theatre.

There is an incredible difference between watching a horror story in the safety of your own home, with a TV screen between you and the story, and being present when the story is physically unfolding around you. The stage production includes characters walking through the audience, putting you within reach of the action, and some set-pieces that are chilling just to even remember. For me, it's the closest thing to being "real" and "intense" as it gets.

I won't soon forget the image of a rocking chair moving on its own in one scene, only to appear again later with the eponymous woman in black sitting in it as it moves, then rising in one fluid motion out of the chair and walking across the stage.

TELL US ABOUT YOUR CONTRIBUTION TO OUR BOOK. WHAT WAS THE INSPIRATION?

My contribution is taken from real life. It's an event that occurred to me (and my wife, although she was blissfully asleep throughout the whole thing) and is the one time in my life that I was the most scared I have ever been. While part of me can think of a rational explanation to explain what happens, there's still enough doubt in my mind that it was something far from mundane.

WHAT DO YOU LOVE ABOUT THE GENRE OF HORROR?

Horror breaks the rules of other genres, and that's why I love it so much. Mundane drama in its various forms plays by the rules of the real world. I get far too much of the real world every day as it is, so it's not something I look for in fiction. I turn to fiction to be excited, to be surprised, and if there's a good amount of scares along the way, all the better.

The way I see it, horror sets up an environment you may well think you are familiar with at the start, but then quickly pulls the rug out from under you, radically changing what you thought you knew about the story. You're left surprised, shocked, and wondering just what is possible in the events to come. That grabs me and keeps me hooked more than any other genre can ever hope to achieve.

What is some of your favorite horror literature? Favorite Author?

My favorite horror author is definitely James Herbert. What appeals to me so much about his work is that while all his books were horror, he interwove elements of other genres to provide a different feeling to a lot of his books. *The Spear* includes elements of a spy thriller. *The Fog* has a disaster movie-like quality. *Shrine* has a distinctly religious theme. *Domain* is post-apocalyptic.

Herbert wrote my all-time favorite novel, *Haunted*. It's a fairly short book, but one that packs a lot in between its covers. As the title suggests, it's a ghost story, about a parapsychologist that debunks claims of hauntings. Without spoiling it for those that haven't read it (to whom I wholeheartedly recommend this book!), it has a twist that is unlike any other ghost story I've read, and one that puts it head and shoulders above the rest for me. Echoing what I wrote above about why I love horror so much—I live for those moments when the rug gets pulled out from under me, and *Haunted* does exactly that.

What are some of your influences?

I tend to find most of my influences come from literature (in particular, Lovecraft and Poe) and film (the works of Nigel Kneale, the classic Hammer and Amicus productions, and some more recent "extreme" films such as *Martyrs*).

What is your favorite Halloween treat?

Halloween wasn't really a big thing for me when growing up here in the U.K. I think I can count on one hand how many trick-or-treaters visited our house in 20 years. In that context, ANY treat I managed to get at that time would have been much appreciated!

You are hosting the perfect Halloween movie marathon. What are the films you choose and why?

I think it would have to be films set around that time of year to really qualify. Plus, there really should be some titles in there for the kids to enjoy. They'll probably be awake for the start of the marathon. Eventually, they'll head to bed, and then give the adults a chance to enjoy something a little more grown up.

For the Kids:
- *The House with a Clock in Its Walls* (2018)—I haven't seen a kid's movie that good in a while. Who could possibly refuse a bit of necromancy in their family entertainment?
- *Halloweentown* (1998)—I thought it was pretty good, and it's a favorite of my wife's, so I'd probably not survive the night if it didn't make an appearance on the list.
- *Hocus Pocus* (1993)—Another of my wife's favorites, but I've got to admit, those sisters have a pretty good surname (I'm an only child, before you ask!).

For the Adults:
- *Halloween* (1978)—The John Carpenter classic. How could this NOT appear on this list?
- *Trick 'r Treat* (2007)—I love a good anthology, and this one has some nice moments.
- *Halloween 3: Season of the Witch* (1982)—Definitely the best entry in the series in my opinion, so saving the best till last.

IF YOU COULD CONTINUE ANY HORROR STORY (BOOK OR FILM), WHAT WOULD IT BE?

The vast majority of horror films and books I've read have all felt nicely self-contained and complete. However, the one that sticks out in my mind that's been begging (or maybe screaming) for a continuation is Clive Barker's *Cabal* (filmed by the author as *Nightbreed*). Both the book and the film end on an unresolved note, with so much more left to be done, but the reader and viewer never get to see it happen. I'd love to see what happens to the survivors that escaped the fall of Midian. For the moment though, I can only dream.

DESCRIBE THE PERFECT HALLOWEEN.

It would have to be a ghost hunt for me. There's plenty of places that claim to be haunted in the area here, and several of them run ghost hunts overnight on Halloween. What better night of the year is there to try and experience a piece of the paranormal? Of course, if a spirit decided to appear, and my camera was able to capture the image… well, that would be the icing on the cake.

ONE SUMMER NIGHT
IN CHEROKEE

In the summer of 2014, I travelled to the United States from the United Kingdom to propose to my wife-to-be, Tiffany. We originally met back in 2006 when we both attended a convention in Florida where we were both pretending to be vampires. It was a live-action roleplaying game convention—but putting it that way always makes us chuckle and it usually makes the listener do a bit of a double-take. Over time, our relationship grew and eventually I plucked up the courage to ask her to marry me. It only took eight years—a fact she often reminds me of.

In the lead-up to the big day, I arranged to spend a couple of weeks with Tiffany. She was living in North Carolina at the time and wanted to take me to some of the places she had visited when she was growing up. Her parents often took her camping in the Great Smoky Mountains around Cherokee, and she knew the place well. We rented a car and she drove us out there. I made sure I carried the ring I intended to give her discretely kept on me at all times, or at the very least within arm's reach. There was no way I was going to lose it just days before the proposal!

Rather than camping (as Tiffany knew I liked my creature comforts) we decided that our plan was to find a room at one of the many Bed and Breakfast establishments on Tsali Boulevard (Highway 441) that headed north from the center of Cherokee. Many of these backed onto the banks of the Oconaluftee River where Tiffany had frequently played during her childhood visits.

Even though Tiffany was adamant that finding a room would be easy, we drove past one sign after another that all declared the same thing—"No Vacancy".

As we came to the end of what we thought were all of our options, we passed a hotel on the left-hand side of the road. It was part of a chain of hotels seen all across the country and certainly stood out compared to all the other buildings we'd seen on the road up until this point. Three stories tall, all the front-facing rooms appeared to have balconies that flanked the main entrance in the middle of the building. Its grand appearance implied it might be expensive, but it was apparent it was our only option at that point.

Tiffany was a little disappointed that the hotel wasn't closer to the river, as it stood on the opposite side of the road, but nevertheless we pulled into the car park and within minutes had secured a room. It was a little more expensive than we'd budgeted for compared to the rates for a typical Bed and Breakfast, but our room was spacious and comfortable. There wasn't anything that one would call "special" about the room. It was a standard hotel room layout. The bathroom was immediately next to the main door, it was pretty normal in every respect. We had two large beds to choose from and a large TV on the opposite wall. As far as I was concerned, it was money well spent.

After dropping our bags off in the room, we took a drive to one of the places in Cherokee that she knew I wanted to visit—the local casino. I've always enjoyed a game of poker and consider myself to be a moderately good texas hold 'em player and had put aside some money specifically for the occasion. We spent a while waiting for a seat to become available at one of the tables but eventually my time came.

Lady luck was on my side that night and an Ace-high flush on the river earned me a $505 pot when several players had gone all-in ahead of me. That paid for the car rental, the hotel and left us with a little spending money for the next couple of days. We left the casino on a high note and went back to the hotel. It had been a long day by that point, and we were both ready for some rest.

What happened a few hours later has remained vividly in my memory ever since that night. I suspect it will remain that way until the day I die. Terror has a very acute way of making a lasting impression.

Having set the scene, I now want to take the opportunity to reassure you, dear reader, that I am not a person that has a history of "seeing things." In fact, the only time I ever hallucinated was in 2007. I'd flown out to Tombstone, Arizona, to take part in a poker game that was being held by the live-action roleplaying game society that both me and Tiffany were members of. Luck was nowhere to be found that night. Not only did the cards hate me, but I was rather ill throughout the trip, having picked something up from a visitor to the office where I worked a few days before I flew out to the States.

When I eventually got home, I was diagnosed with borderline pneumonia and spent much of the next couple of weeks in bed recovering. However, in Tombstone, with that diagnosis still a couple of days away and no medication to help me through the night after the poker game, I had a terrible fever and could hardly sleep. With the same vivid recollection of what happened that night in Cherokee, I remember my hallucination in that motel room in Tombstone. The door to the room silently opened and a procession of five figures in hooded robes, their arms crossed in front of them entered the room. The third figure, the one in the middle of the row of five, held a huge block of ice on a purple pillow in front of him. The figure held it in much the same way one would carry a crown to a coronation. The five figures glided silently through the room and into the bathroom, and that was the last I saw of them.

I remember how ill I was that night in Tombstone. Thankfully, I haven't been that ill since, and I was certainly in good health when me and Tiffany visited Cherokee, so I cannot explain away what I saw in the hotel room as being a fever-dream or hallucination.

It was the middle of the night when I woke up. I suspect it was the result of Tiffany moving beside me. A movement at the end of the bed caught my eye. Tiffany was there, naked, her long dark hair flowing down her back. She was looking away from me so I couldn't see her face, and she was walking casually towards the bathroom. She went inside the bathroom, which I thought at the time was a little odd. There was a little bit of light coming through the curtains from the road outside, as we had a front-facing room, but it couldn't have been enough to see by in the bathroom.

The bed was comfortable and now that Tiffany had gone to the bathroom, I had it all to myself. I stretched out my arms to both sides of me, hoping to enjoy the space for a few moments. While my left arm dangled off the edge of the bed, my right arm hit something hard. At first, I thought it was the bunched-up duvet, or perhaps a very hard pillow, but quickly I realized it couldn't be, it was too hard to be either of those. In the dim light, I could see Tiffany's sleeping face pointed towards me as she still lay in bed. My right arm had collided with her elbow. The question came into my mind no more than a second later, as I sat wide-eyed in bed, looking towards the bathroom door: who had I seen at the end of my bed?

The rational part of me quickly started to analyze what was happening. I had only thought it was Tiffany because the figure had similarly long hair. From behind, in the dark, that had been an easy assumption to make (especially as it was only supposed to be the two of us in the room!). But it had to be *someone* as I had *definitely* seen them. This wasn't a figment of my imagination or the confusion of some half-formed dream with reality in the moment of my waking from slumber. I was positive that I had seen someone in our room, and that person was now in our bathroom, waiting in the dark.

I don't know exactly how long I lay in bed, gripped by terror, staring at the open bathroom door, waiting for someone (or something) to emerge from the darkness. My mind raced with other questions. What if it was someone that had broken into the room to rob us? I couldn't see my wallet in the dark. Had they gone through it and taken the winnings from the poker game? Maybe it was someone that heard us talking about it when we got back to the hotel and had waited until we were both asleep to finally make their move? But, if that was the case, why were they naked? It didn't make any sense—no-one breaks into a hotel room naked. Likewise, what kind of burglar hides in the bathroom when they've been seen, putting them in a position with no way out? Surely, they would have made straight for the main door and run out. It didn't make any sense, but all the time I kept thinking that they were still in the bathroom.

Running through the various possibilities and discounting

them, one by one, I finally settled upon one explanation that I couldn't build a strong enough counterargument for. What if the figure I had seen had been a ghost? It seemed ridiculous at first. As far I could tell, the building looked pretty new. When we pulled up, the exterior looked bright and fresh with no sign of wear and tear. The rooms were tidy, the corridors showed no signs of age. Weren't hauntings supposed to happen in old places, places with history? That said, how many people had passed through this hotel over the years? I read somewhere once that deaths in hotels were not as rare as people think. How many had potentially died here? Was this a guest that had checked in and never left?

Once that thought had entered my mind, I couldn't get it out again. I just lay there, hoping that whatever (rather than whoever) was in the bathroom stayed there. If I'd had the courage, I should have got up to turn on the light and see for myself if there was anything in there, but I simply couldn't move.

Eventually, tiredness must have taken its toll and I fell back to sleep. When I woke the next morning, strengthened by the sunlight pouring through the window, I found my wallet untouched with all the winnings from the casino still present, and the bathroom was completely empty. The main door was still locked and the door guard latch still in place. It seemed pretty obvious to me; no-one had come through that door besides us last night.

When Tiffany was awake, I told her about what I had seen during the night. She replied, saying that she had woken up at some point as well, only to find a native woman standing beside the bed, looking down at her through long dark hair. There wasn't any look of hostility in her face, Tiffany said, she was just looking at her in bed. I was stunned and still am not quite sure what to make of it, even after the years that have passed. Could it really have been the same figure? After all, I never saw their face, but the long hair sounded the same.

We stayed in the hotel for a second night after visiting various places in the area Tiffany wanted to show me. Even though I spent what seemed like hours staring into the dark, scared of what might appear again, much to my relief, nothing happened that night. When we finally checked out, Tiffany asked the member of staff at the front desk if they had ever had any guests report any ghost sightings to them. The member of staff was perplexed but shook their head, saying that they weren't aware of any. I still remember Tiffany's excited reply to that before she went on to explain: "Well, you have one now!"

A few days later, we travelled to the Fort Raleigh National Historic Site, the location of the famous Roanoke Colony. In the Elizabethan Gardens there, I finally gave Tiffany the ring I'd been carrying around with me all the time around Cherokee. We married early the following year and have been happy together ever since—especially as neither of us has seen anyone else standing at the end of our bed or looking at us when we've woken up in the middle of the night.

CHRISTIAN STOKES

Outsider, Loner, Outlaw: These are the roles that define Christian Stokes. From an undercover biker cop in *Monster* featuring an Academy Award winning performance from Charlize Theron, to an intimidating mob enforcer going through cigarette withdrawal opposite of Brad Dourif and Kenny Johnson in the indy feature, *Few Options*, Christian has embraced these characters with intensity and a raw, talented grit. He continues to find the hearts of darkness that lurk within these men in projects far and wide.

Christian Stokes was raised in East Texas and grew up the oldest son of a firefighter. He credits his laid-back, easy-going manner to growing up with his grandparents and learning the value of hard work and determination. That focus has led Christian to working steadily in show business for 28 years. He is an eight-year veteran of the Hollywood film scene, having performed with such actors as Jennifer Garner, Matthew McConaughey, Bruce Dern, and Sylvester Stallone. Some of his other highlighted credits include *Doom Patrol, Escape Plan, Revolution, No Ordinary Family, Leverage: Redemption*, and *Bernie*, starring Jack Black.

Christian has been interested in the Haunt Industry ever since his father designed haunted houses for the local Junior Chamber of Commerce in Christian's hometown when he was a child. Christian has been involved in the haunt industry off and on for 24 years and he currently serves as the creative director for New Orlean's iconic haunted Halloween attraction The Mortuary

Haunted House located at the dead end of Canal Street, right next to the famous City of the Dead!

Christian recently finished filming a supporting role in the highly anticipated horror feature, *Five Nights at Freddy's*, based on the highly popular video game of the same name, and is looking forward to its October 2023 release.

WHAT DO YOU LOVE ABOUT THE GENRE OF HORROR?

Ever since I was a kid, I remember going to the movies and watching *Friday the 13th* and *Halloween*. Nothing like the modern version of telling a ghost story around the campfire. Although, the campfire in this case is the communal experience of a movie theatre and the ghost story is told visually on the cinema screen!

WHAT IS SOME OF YOUR FAVORITE HORROR LITERATURE?

I was introduced to horror literature by reading Stephen King's *Salems Lot* when I was young. Nowadays, I read (or listen) to almost anything King publishes!

WHAT ARE SOME OF YOUR INFLUENCES?

I did a book report my senior year of high school on H.P. Lovecraft. It was a chance choosing as I was rushed to pick an author and I wanted to do something a little different. Boy, did that book report have a lasting impression. Most of my themes revolve around something terrible and strange, lurking just behind the curtain of sanity. Also, *Poltergeist* and films that deal with hauntings and supernatural horrors, like the *Conjuring* films and such, truly resonate with my "ghost story" appreciation.

WHAT IS YOUR FAVORITE HALLOWEEN TREAT?

Rice Crispy Treats. Hands down!

YOU ARE HOSTING THE PERFECT HALLOWEEN MOVIE MARATHON, WHAT ARE THE FILMS YOU CHOOSE AND WHY?

You know, the best Halloween movie marathon lasts at least 13 days, and maybe even the full 31 if I have time in October. I like to mix films like *Friday the 13th, Poltergeist,* and *Halloween,* with old classics like Abbot and Costello monster films and early Universal Monster movies. And then, add a splattering of recent stuff, like *The Conjuring, Nope,* and *Black Phone.* A good marathon is a roller coaster ride, starting light and ending with the movie *Halloween* on Halloween!

DESCRIBE THE PERFECT HALLOWEEN.

The perfect Halloween usually ends up with me being in New Orleans, one of the coolest cities to be in during the Halloween festivities… I like to experience a Haunted House attraction, followed by a real life, supernatural experience such as a ghost tour or touring an old abandoned haunted prison. If we survive that, we finish the evening wrapped in a blanket watching a movie with a steady supply of popcorn and candy!!

IF YOU COULD CONTINUE ANY HORROR STORY FROM LITERATURE OR FILM, WHAT WOULD IT BE?

I'd like to see what John Carpenter would have done next with *The Fog* … or, speaking of John Carpenter, what would the next chapter of *The Thing* hold?

AS A DESIGNER, EXPLAIN YOUR PROCESS. WHERE DO YOU DRAW INSPIRATION AND HOW DO YOU CHOOSE YOUR NEXT STEPS?

I lean heavily into pop culture. I also enjoy seeing what is new at Transworld. I walk up and down the convention center and let my imagination run wild. I will create several story skeletons and synopses that I submit to the owner of the Mortuary. Every year, we try to link the current theme to the one before it and so on, so we have one continual story thread that dates back to our original season 17 years ago. He narrows it down to a pair and I go to work creating a legend based on these two themes. Once he tells me which he prefers, we go into research and start bouncing ideas and designs between the department heads and create a truly collaborative production year in and year out.

WHEN WAS THE LAST TIME YOU WERE GENUINELY SCARED BY SOMETHING SOMEONE CREATED?

After being involved in this industry for all these years, I have become quite desensitized to the jump scares and the loud noises and light specials. In short, I haven't been scared by anyone/anything created in many years. As such, I offer $100 to the first scare actor to make me jump every year. Still waiting!

TELL US ABOUT YOUR CONTRIBUTION TO OUR BOOK. WHAT WAS THE INSPIRATION?

I am telling you a story about the Mortuary and how it is an actual HAUNTED, haunted house. In this story, I relate my own supernatural experiences that I've had in the place recently. I was inspired by the fact that we had several haunt owners from around the country tour the Mortuary in 2021 for The Legendary Haunt Tour. I was asked to give them some background on the attraction and the building, and once I started relating these experiences as they were waiting to enter the attraction, I noticed a definite shift in their mood as they prepared to enter the haunt. When they were finished, they sought me out and told me that my experience completely enhanced their overall enjoyment and really creeped them out. And so, the stories I've experienced in the Mortuary scream to be told!

THE HAUNTED HAUNTED HOUSE

I've been involved in the haunt industry now for about 23 years. I loved Halloween as a kid and really enjoyed going the extra mile with makeup and costuming when I was in college. As an entertainer, I did a couple of Halloween Shows in the early 2000s at Busch Gardens Tampa Bay and Universal Studios Orlando, including a couple of classic Bill and Ted Shows at Halloween Horror Nights. However, I first participated as a scare actor at Six Flags Magic Mountain for Fright Nights after I moved to Los Angeles to pursue acting and stunt work.

Years passed, and I found myself living in New Orleans, Louisiana in early 2011. I had a friend of mine moving in with me and we were looking for a job for him to step into to help with his share of the rent. It was mid-September and we drove past a billboard touting The Mortuary Haunted House. A haunted house! That would be a perfect place to start looking for a new gig for my new roomie.

I found the phone number online. I began to reminisce about my early Haunt fun and decided I wanted to jump back into the world of Haunt, myself! I left a message in regard to the two of us. The next day, the owner, Jeff Borne, received our message and set up a meeting. He hired my buddy, a seasoned L.A. actor, to play one of the icons for that year's house. I told Jeff about my experience running and directing various stunt shows over the years, so he hired me to be the haunt director.

The attraction, The Mortuary, is an old mansion that served as an actual mortuary at the turn of the 20th century. Thousands of bodies were treated in the building's basement level embalming room. (NOTE: A basement is quite rare in New Orleans because of the amount of flooding the city receives! A basement quickly can become a swimming pool if situated in the wrong part of town!) The building is located at the end of Canal Street and is nestled and resting right up next to New Orlean's famed City of the Dead cemeteries. There are one million graves within a square mile of the attraction.

I seem to remember that first year we were doing a Bloody Mary theme. As I made my rounds and worked with the haunt actors, I began to hear stories, here and there, about the house. About its legends and its ghostly denizens. Apparently, and not too surprisingly, considering the house's somewhat morbid history, the Mortuary was actually haunted! An actual HAUNTED, Haunted House. How apropos!

Not that I didn't believe that there weren't things that go bump in the night, but I took everything with a grain of salt, of course. Seeing is believing, right? I did see things when I was a kid, but it was in that time in my life when I wasn't sure if what I saw was real or the product of an overactive imagination. I had never made up my mind about what was or was not out there in terms of the supernatural… I am a man of faith, so I do believe there are things under heaven and earth that defy our description, but hey… this was a haunted house experience. No need to get into a philosophical Gordian Knott concerning the existence of actual ghosts and goblins. One thing I knew for sure though, scaring people was a whole lot of FUN!

Working at the Mortuary for over ten years as director, casting manager and eventually creative director, I had heard it all. I had heard stories of actors seeing an old lady's wrinkled and disembodied head superimposed over a mannequin head in our terrifying clown room. I heard stories of people who saw things moving in and out of shadows. Several people described seeing the same top-hat toting figure loitering in the basement halls in different places throughout the house in between guest pulses at the height of Haunt Season. Several

employees said they couldn't work in certain places in the house because of the oppressive feeling they experienced after being previously placed there. Some of these employees outright quit. I had even seen a picture of a full-bodied apparition of a little girl (that one made Zak Bagan's Ghost Adventures), but I wasn't the one that took it, so there was always the shadow of doubt.

Throughout the years, despite all of this, I had never seen a single thing. I had even asked Jeff on more than one occasion about it. He always gave me a knowing smile and a wink, like he was letting me in on some secret, inside joke. He'd tell me a story about a shadow person that had moved his bed across the room one night while he was staying overnight at the mansion, but the way he said it lacked conviction. Almost like he didn't believe it himself. Or didn't want to believe it. Or … MAYBE, I surmised, it was something else entirely … maybe it was all part of a brilliant plan! Perhaps, a brilliant marketing campaign designed to make everyone believe that a functioning haunted house was actually HAUNTED, in order to create a next level experience, where the guests would never know if they were screaming at an actor who was skillfully wrapped in shadow and atmosphere, or, if indeed, it was an authentic insubstantial creature of shadow, reaching for the paying customer from beyond the grave!

What an ingenious idea! I was blown away and completely immersed myself into the inside joke, even going so far as to create 'events' that would mystify the employees and make them spread the Mortuary's infamy to all corners of the Big Easy. (ASIDE TO ANY OF MY CAST READING THIS: Remember the haunted wheelchair that would roll all over the house? That was me!)

It felt so good being a part of the initiated, one of the few folks that knew the Unspoken Secret to the Mortuary. I began to return Jeff's knowing winks and relating all of the various stories over the years to anyone who would listen. I now understood what the 'legend' of the Mortuary was all about.

And boy was I wrong, because it FINALLY happened to me!

In September of 2021, I had just moved to Atlanta to pursue opportunities in my film and stunt career, and I was staying at the Mortuary in order that I could physically be in New Orleans for that year's Haunt Season. There are a couple of suites hidden in semi-secret corners of the house where the staff can stay overnight on late nights or during hell week, that last two weeks leading to

Halloween where the action is non-stop!

I decided to set up shop in the Casket Room, one of the themed rooms in the attraction. It had one of the most comfortable couches I had ever had the pleasure of taking a nap on. I wanted to keep the suites open in case anyone needed to stay and, with that comfy couch, I was perfectly fine staying down there.

My roommates were a blood covered life-sized statue that reminded me of the iconic scene from *Carrie* where the title character was completely drenched in blood, a mad scientist wearing a gas mask with his nose and mandible missing where the mask attached, and an authentic wooden casket on the top of which Carrie rested in her bloodstained glory! Most people I know thought I was crazy for CHOOSING to sleep down there, but I wasn't concerned. These were our creations. There was nothing to fear! Or so I thought!

One night, after a particularly busy evening at the attraction, I was sitting on that comfy couch, collecting my thoughts and trying to catch my breath. All of the actors had just gotten out of makeup and left, and the other manager, Lance, had just said goodbye and made his way home as well. I was zoning out, flipping through my phone, as you do after a crazy night of haunting. Just sitting there on zombie mode, enjoying the peace and quiet … when something

sat down on the couch beside me. I could not only see the depression where this invisible force sat, but I could physically feel it move across me and drape its legs over mine, like a child would when sitting beside you. And partially on you!

I was stunned! I know what I was feeling and seeing, but I was completely surprised and at a loss. When that happens to me, I usually use humor to help me find my True North once more. So, I said out loud, half-jokingly, half terrified, "You can't sit here! There's a chair right over there." And as soon as I said that it got up. I could feel it leave. And just like that, I had my first experience in the house, ten years after I first started working there.

I sat there for the next few minutes, a little bit dumbstruck and immediately second-guessing myself. I had already begun to question whether or not what I had experienced had actually happened or if it was just that I was so tired. I pulled the covers up extra high that night and slept facing the inside of the couch, because, despite my attempt at rationalization, I knew what I had experienced had to be real.

I told a few people what had happened the next day, and to be fair, none of them seemed surprised. I even told Jeff. Now, his wink and knowing smile seemed different to me. Like, THIS was the secret club I was always supposed to eventually become a part of.

And, though I still was questioning my experience, the next thing that happened would confirm everything!

Only a few days later, while sleeping on that comfy couch, I woke up at around 9:00 am to the sound of a woman crying. It was a terrible, deep sobbing kind of grief that comes from someone truly suffering. The door to the patio was only a few feet away and it sounded like it was coming from outside. As I sprang up to check on the person outside, the closer I came to the door, I quickly realized that the sobbing was not coming from outside, but from inside the house, deeper into the front part of the mansion. I was confused, as I was certain that I was the only one in the house. My hair started standing up on my arm as I realized this may be another supernatural encounter! I made my way to the room where the weeping was coming from. The only thing between me and the room was a curtain. As I reached for the curtain, I remember thinking that I knew I was going to look inside and that I wasn't going to find anyone there. And as soon as the thought entered my mind, the weeping stopped.

I entered the room and nothing... no person... no crying... nothing. I asked out loud if there was anyone there and if they needed help. Now, let's be honest here. I was pretty creeped out myself and wanted to leave that room. I already knew the answer! So, after asking the question, I turned around and attempted to high tail it out of there... I say attempted, because, the moment I started through the curtain again, something from behind me... in that room that I was in ... hissed in my left ear like an angry cat. THAT sent chills down my spine. As a completely involuntary reflex, I yelled out, "Don't get mad at me! I heard you crying, and I came looking to help." And with that, I made a beeline back to my little area!

You better believe I told everyone about that experience. And I did not second guess nor question what had happened this go around. I was wide awake and fully conscious. I've experienced a few things since then, but nothing quite as 'in your face.' Televisions coming on in a locked room. Doors locking inexplicably. All of this can be explained away as being on a timer or the wood swelling from being wet from the rain … But I can tell you that nowadays, I sleep in the suite, and not on that comfy couch! It's still a comfy couch, but I can't sleep as well with one eye open!

And now, I am quite certain that the brilliant marketing ploy that I convinced myself of was the only true figment of my own mind concerning the house. After these experiences that I have described above, I am 100 percent convinced that the Mortuary Haunted House is a legitimately HAUNTED house! Don't believe me? Come see for yourself this Halloween!!!

J. MICHAEL RODDY

J. Michael Roddy began his entertainment career as an actor. His encyclopedic knowledge of pop culture brought him opportunities to write and direct. He has been a prevalent member of the design team for Halloween Horror Nights at Universal Studios. There he created and implemented over one-hundred haunted attractions and scarezones.

He has also created successful shows and attractions for Walt Disney Creative Entertainment involving *Star Wars, Frozen, Pixar, Marvel*, and Disney Cruise Line. He was also a producer on 2011s award-winning documentary *The Shark is Still Working: The Impact & Legacy of Jaws* and 2017s award-winning *MonsterKids*. In 2018, he won a Rondo Hattan Award for Best Documentary.

He recently formed Roddy Creative LLC where he provides creative writing and directing for live shows, attractions, exhibits and marquee events. He is also the creator of *MonsterKids*—a podcast that delves into the positive influence of horror genre on culture. He lives in Central Florida with his wife, two kids, three dogs, and two cats.

WHAT DO YOU LOVE ABOUT THE GENRE OF HORROR?

The horror genre is an intermingling of three elements: fear, anxiety, and relief. The sense of foreboding that sets you up and the piercing impact that the nightmare is real are followed by the resolution and then calm.

I have been a horror fan since my earliest memories of discovering stories. The anticipation and excitement and the rush of adrenaline led me to darker stories and films. I love that the genre is cathartic. You make it through a great book, film, or piece of theatre, and you feel you have survived and overcome. Maybe this helps us in some way face our fears and be prepared for them. When a good story has you, and you are there with the characters, you feel the threat and danger. You allow yourself to immerse yourself and suspend disbelief… but at the end, the lights come on and you are safe. I fell in love with that feeling very early in my life. I love that feeling, that unnerving yet slow approach of dread, a creepiness that crawls up your neck. Then, when the tension is taut comes the blinding exposure, the dark veil lifted… BOOM!

Do you fight or succumb? Regardless of the outcome, it ends. The calm is welcome as a respite of the fear, but then you realize it is really the echo of it all. All is back to normal, but the memory of that horrific moment can creep back time and again sparked by a sound, a shadow, or even the wind.

My passion for story is firmly rooted in the tales of ghosts, monsters, and the supernatural. Sure, I enjoy all stories, from adventure to romance to fantasy, but it is the tomes of terror that I find my most visited.

"He who is not every day conquering some fear has not learned the secret of life."

--Ralph Waldo Emerson

WHAT IS SOME OF YOUR FAVORITE HORROR LITERATURE?

Stephen King, Ray Bradbury, Robert McCammon, HP Lovecraft, and Richard Matheson.

If you love Halloween, read the works of Ray Bradbury. If you have not read *The Halloween Tree,* then put this book down and go read that immediately. It conjures all the feelings of childhood in autumn and is a history of Halloween as well.

Stephen King's *Pet Semetary* comes to mind as one of the books that completely had me in its grip from beginning to end. Gage was a terrible creation, and the rug gets pulled out from under you several times. I still believe that it is one of the scariest books ever written.

Lovecraft is also such a powerful author. His descriptive passages of slimy, black organisms in many cases make no sense in the conformity of the mind and allow you to try and visualize which then creates terror. Lovecraft created the worst things that reside in the dark, ancient creeps that are black as pitch and burrow into your sanity to rip it apart.

I am also a fan of Robert McCammon's *Mystery Walk* and *Clive Barker's Coldheart Canyon: A Hollywood Ghost Story*

WHO ARE SOME OF YOUR INFLUENCES?

John Carpenter, Steven Spielberg, Houdini, Tom Savini, Greg Nicotero.

These men shaped stories through their talents as directors, make-up men, and magicians. All of them are Masters of the illusion.

Steven Spielberg: *Jaws* continues to be an example of perfect visual storytelling and how effective your imagination can be. Think about those yellow barrels and that theme. They complete the shark's image.

John Carpenter: The best horror director. His films are textbooks in how to generate tension and fear. I love them all. And his music is always playing when I write.

Houdini: He spent a lifetime debunking spiritualism, yet is still so connected with the supernatural.

Tom Savini: The modern-day showman, he is everything I want to be. Magician, make-up artist, actor, and director.

Greg Nicotero: He is our modern day Monsterkid. Like Savini before him, he took what we all love and continues to drive the fun of being scared.

WHAT IS YOUR FAVORITE HALLOWEEN TREAT?
Halloween M & M's and Almond Joy bars.

YOU ARE HOSTING THE PERFECT HALLOWEEN MOVIE MARATHON. WHAT ARE THE FILMS YOU CHOOSE AND WHY?
Halloween TV is as much of a crucial part of my celebration as watching a great scary movie. This list represents my must watch programming for the week of Halloween. But if I could do it in one great marathon, here is how it would happen. It would be great to put this together for a group of friends. We would start around 5 PM, just as the sky was turning orange and the night was approaching. There would be pizza, treats, and music. We would play *Clue*. I would also show short spooky-themed films that I have collected over the years including Greg Nicotero's amazing tribute to the classics of horror, *The United Monster Talent Agency, and* Michael Dougherty's animated *Season's Greetings*. Joe Bob Briggs would be our host.

You do believe in the Great Pumpkin don't you?

It's the Great Pumpkin, Charlie Brown
If you don't know why this kicks off the list, we have nothing to talk about. I believe in the Great Pumpkin. I believe that on Halloween night, the Great Pumpkin rises from his pumpkin patch and delivers toys to all the good little boys and girls.

An episode of *The Addams Family.*

I want to live in that house.

"Haunted"

The *Happy Days* Halloween episode from 1974. I love the simplicity of this era, and this episode has it all.

"The Haunted House"

The season four episode of *The Andy Griffith Show* from 1963 is perfectly creepy and hilarious. The old Rimshaw place is astounding in its design with revolving doors and paintings with eyes that follow you around the room. Don Knotts and Jim Nabors are comedic artists, and this episode allows them to shine.

"Cat's Paw" and "The Wolf in the Fold"

These Halloween episodes of the classic *Star Trek* series are both absolutely chilling.

Abbott & Costello Meet Frankenstein

It doesn't get better than this spookfest from 1948. All of the monsters are represented and act accordingly. It has all of the favorite tropes of the Universal classic monster films with the delightful humor of Bud Abbott and Lou Costello. The best thing is that the monsters are never made fun of. They are scary and threatening.

John Carpenter's *Halloween*

This is a true masterpiece of suspense and foreboding. The music, the visuals, and the tone all combine to capture what I think is the scarier side of the holiday. I didn't get to see *Halloween* until it aired on TV the weekend that *Halloween II* opened in theatres, but I was aware of the story and the TV ads had scared me in 1979 with the promise of the night He came home.

Night of The Living Dead

I first saw this on a PBS station on Halloween night 1979. Halloween that year was on a Wednesday, and with the looming expectation of school the next morning, all of the trick 'r treaters had stopped early. The night was pitch black and cold. I nestled into bed and watched it on a tiny 13-inch screen. I can still remember the opening, the music, everything. And when you discover that the ghouls were eating people… absolutely terrifying.

PARKING
FOR
CEMETERY
VISITORS
DAYLIGHT HOU

IF YOU COULD CONTINUE ANY HORROR STORY, WHAT WOULD IT BE?

I have always wanted to continue the story of John Carpenter's *The Fog*. I have a pretty solid concept that had Blake and his crew returning to Antonio Bay 30 years after the events of the first film. I also have a lot of pieces to a sequel to *Frankenstein* that would continue the creature's journey, but there has been so much already. I have always wanted to try my hand at a revision of *The Most Dangerous Game* as well.

AS A DESIGNER OF HORROR THEATRE OR EXPERIENCES, EXPLAIN YOUR PROCESS.

My process always starts with the connection. I always look for ways to connect the guest or reader to the situation. I love being an audience and put myself through all of it before I start to commit it to design. First, I look for the theme, the essence of the idea. Next, I figure out the location and the history. Where do I want to venture… a graveyard, a carnival, a funeral parlor? What happened? Then, I plunk the audience in the middle of that moment and let the ghosts have at them.

When creating a Haunt, I always start with what role we are asking the guest to play in the experience. I believe that mazes and haunted houses are moments in a bigger story. If I had no restriction on time, I would create an entire story presented as moments of theatre, but usually, you only have so much space, time, and budget, so I create an immense backstory that I can explain through video, sound, and setting, and then put the guest into that story as an active participant at a specific time.

WHEN IS THE LAST TIME YOU WERE GENUINELY SCARED BY SOMETHING SOMEONE CREATED?

From a movie standpoint, the following films have done a pretty effective job at scaring me. *Hereditary* disturbed me greatly. *The Host* on Netflix. Mike Flannagan is becoming one of my favorite new filmmakers. *The House on Haunted Hill, Doctor Sleep, Hush, Gerald's Game…* I would love to spend a few minutes chatting with him.

TELL US ABOUT YOUR CONTRIBUTION TO OUR BOOK. WHAT WAS THE INSPIRATION?

I have included a recollection of working at one of the greatest haunts I ever experienced: Terror on Church Street. Allow me to transport you back nearly two decades. As I look back on that fateful chapter of my life, I do so with a mixture of nostalgia and trepidation, knowing that some experiences are destined to linger long after the curtains have fallen and the lights have dimmed. And though time may have dulled the edges of those memories, the chill of Terror on Church Street still sends shivers down my spine, reminding me that some haunts are best left undisturbed.

DESCRIBE THE PERFECT HALLOWEEN.

I want the coolness in the air, the orange dusk, and the deep blue midnight. The crackling of the fire and the hint of supernatural in the air. Then, there's a crunch of fallen leaves somewhere in the distance. Was that a cackle overhead?

If I could have my Mom back for one more Halloween, I would let her see how her sacrifice and love inspired me to do the same.

The perfect Halloween would involve friends, food, and fear. There would be a cold chill in the air and the smell of crispness. There would be giggles and screams and a bit of creeping foreboding to the sun setting. There would be a bright full moon and the promise of the supernatural.

Halloween seems to be changing from what was so special for me… the feel, the chill, the senses. It has become somewhat melancholy as I keep looking backward into the autumns or my youth. It seems the innocence of allowing yourself to be scared by folklore and traditions has been replaced by cynicism. I hope that we can get that back for future generations.

A HAUNTING IN A HAUNT

In February of 1993, I started working at a haunted attraction in Orlando called Terror on Church Street. Terror on Church Street opened to guests in 1991, featuring two floors of experiences based on the popular horror characters and scary situations of the genre. The experience was pulsed, meaning that guests were separated by time so that each experience within could reset.

The origins of this macabre attraction were far from sinister. In fact, they traced back to a humble stage production featuring local actors. What began as a modest theatrical endeavor soon snowballed into an international sensation, thanks to the vision of two men: Fernando Quenard and Ignacio Brieva.

These pioneers of fright had been inspired by Pasaje Del Terror, an interactive horror walk-thru that captivated audiences in cities across the globe. Determined to bring a similar experience to the United States, Quenard and Brieva joined forces to make their terrifying dream a reality.

Under the watchful eye of Mr. Rafael Fondevila and the skilled guidance of the Rivas Brothers, a new entity emerged: "OMEN" (Orlando Monster Enterprise). This production company would serve as the driving force behind "Terror Orlando," orchestrating every scream, every gasp, and every heart-pounding moment of fear.

Using an old Woolworth building in downtown Orlando, they transformed 22,450 square feet using sets, sound and lighting, special effects, and a cast of actors in terrifying costumes and make-up. In an era when haunts were generally staffed by volunteers or minimum-wage teens, Terror was a professional theatrical production. As word spread of the haunted house on Church Street, brave souls from near and far flocked to Orlando in search of nightmare-fueled thrills. With each passing year, the attraction evolved, incorporating cutting-edge effects, spine-chilling scenes, and a cast of performers who brought nightmares to life. When I started at Terror, the creative guidance had transitioned to the real hero of horror for the attraction: David Clevinger. It was his show direction and set design that elevated Terror on Church Street from attraction to a theatrical spectacle of horror.

One of my main jobs was to be a "fisher." The term is from the old days of vaudeville theatre. It is the "fisher's" job to work the crowd, encouraging passersby to buy a ticket and entertain those who wait in a line. I enjoyed working this role quite a lot. David gave me freedom to create characters to try. With David's encouragement, I concocted various characters, from a Jack the Ripper-inspired vampire to a deranged butler reminiscent of Dwight Frye's Renfield. One night, playing a vampire, as I went to bare my fangs at a group of approaching tourists, one of the teeth broke and fell out, clattering across the red paver bricks of church street. The group looked at me. I quickly morphed into Snaggles, the one-toothed vampire with a prominent lisp. One of the main actors that appeared in this role was the late Mike Accord. Mike created a wonderful character name Lon Midnight, and with his boisterous and booming baritone voice and laugh, he was the true face of that building.

Guests lined up around the building, the red neon creating a dark atmosphere. The appropriate music along with Anthony Perkin's narration created a feeling of dread.

Once it was a guest's turn to finally enter, the person would be ushered into the building in a group of eight to ten "bodies" and held in a dimly lit courtyard of a time gone by. With the echoing sounds of horse-drawn carriages rolling along wet cobblestones, wisping fog and lighting from unseen flickering lamplights, the group was immersed in a perfectly creepy, foreboding world.

A pale, dark-eyed, undertaker entered and set the group up with the simple rules for the experience: "Do not run. Do not stop. Do not turn back! Do not touch anyone inside, and *they* will not touch you." With that, guests were ushered into a more claustrophobic scene of a side street. Hanging clothing that they were forced to brush aside created the realism. The street came to a dead end, and the group stood before a large, old door straight out of a Hammer film. "Knock three times," the undertaker bellowed from the distance. There on the door was a large, ornate knocker. The leader of the group had to reach out and use the bronze, carved gargoyle, alerting those beyond with a deep, tapping knell. Chains and locks were heard being opened from behind the wooden door. Then, slowly, the door creaked open, and a robed figure beckoned, face partially revealed through flickering candlelight. He commanded, "Go forward and find yourself standing in the DEAD center of the room."

Once the group moved inside, their eyes started to adjust, and they enjoyed another example of exquisite set design. In the center of the room was a large altar filled with skulls, and candles. The whispers of chants echoed around the dark ceremony. A robed figure appeared and stepped behind the altar. The simulated light from several black candles created an eerie glow and reveled the figure to be a monk. His face was pale and his eyes dark. The robed monk stepped forward, standing above the display, hands outreached toward the guests.

"We are the eternal dwellers of Church Street," the monk's voice would boom,

"and we bid you welcome. You have come here seeking your fate. Within these halls are the things of nightmares, and they are waiting for you. You are about to enter a labyrinth full of ghastly surprises. It is up to you to find your way out, and may your gods protect you."

The monk stepped down from the altar and quickly stared at each member of the group. "You are doomed. You are all doomed," he warned, then moved to one of the cell doors. He forcibly slid the cell open, the attached chains clanging on the bars with a shatteringly unnerving result.

"Go now. Face your fate," he ordered as he forcibly pointed down another hallway, indicating for the group to continue.

Once the group cleared, he slammed the cell door shut with an act of finality. The sound of the metal would ring in their ears.

What followed was a combination of theatre and scares as guests journeyed through room after room of scenarios inspired by haunt classics like *Exorcist, A Nightmare on Elm Street, Psycho, The Texas Chainsaw Massacre* and *Dracula* mixed with classic tropes of mad scientists, zombies, torture, forgotten prisoners, witches, and toxic spills. It ended with the group being chased by a hulking, chainsaw-wielding maniac across a wobbly bridge and through a door that led them into the waiting gift shop. From beginning to end, the show took about 20 minutes.

This was before the unfortunate need for conga lines that ruin most haunt experiences today. Terror was well-acted, well-told, and most importantly, extremely scary. The experience was immensely memorable by both guests and actors alike, and those that were lucky to be a part of it consider it so still be a high-water haunt to this day. But there was also another element to the two-story building on the corner of church street—Terror on Church Street *was* haunted.

I worked at Terror from 1993-1995. It was one of the most rewarding experiences for me. In between groups of guests, I would read about horror and filmmaking through the pages of *Cinemafantastique,* old copies of *Famous Monsters* and great books like *Scare Tatics – The Art, Craft and Trade Secrets of Writing, Producing, and Directing Chillers and Thrillers* by John Russo. I would write ideas on a legal pad or storyboard sequences or create drawings of creatures. A few of us Dwellers were also hopeful film-makers. We would get together to talk of dreams and nightmares and how to create our own horror films while we sat in the dark waiting to terrorize.

Before the story that I am about to recount for you, I had never heard much about the haunting of Church Street. Personally, I believe that there are things that go bump in the night and things that are not of our existence.

Our collective group of fear-making filmmakers came up with a way of using the amazing opportunity afforded us by David Clevinger's sets and production value and put together a project. We would be filming a thirty-minute anthology style show in the style of *Creepshow* and *Tales from the Crypt.* We would write, produce, direct, and star, partnering with Hector Lopez who had access to camera equipment and post-production facilities in nearby Tampa. We would convince David and Omen Productions to let us use the building for our new opus in exchange by using it to also promote Terror, ultimately selling copies in the gift shop. Mike Accord created a new character in the grandest Horror Host fashion named Mr. Darc. He would wrap around the two stories with fun quips and puns. Most of this small team grew up with Horror Hosts and loved the anthology series like *Night Gallery, Twilight Zone*, and both *Tales from the Crypt* and *the Darkside*. One of the stories was called "Full Time." It told the story of an eager horror fan who comes to work at a local haunted attraction only to find that the horrors inside are all too real.

We shot at the building overnight and enjoyed it immensely. We were making a horror show inside a building that had the best sets, working with great actors. Jack directed the segments from a script that I wrote. I also helped with camera and lighting. Hector shared the duties on camera and would be editing. At the end of the filming, quite early in the morning, Hector would take the footage and start the editing from his studio in Tampa.

About a day or two later, Jack and I both met with Hector who was ecstatic. The footage not only looked great, but there was something that showed up that none of us had noticed on set. During one of the shots from the second tale, a young man is being chased through the haunted house as the creatures awaken for their nightly duties. Zombies slowly emerge. The young man runs down, but when the footage came back, we saw something. At first, it looked like someone else was in the hallway. Then we rewound the video and saw that it was transparent. Was it a light reflection? The camera hadn't moved, and this thing followed our actor, swinging out at him in the last moment before disappearing. We continued to frame by frame the footage. As the footage was edited and released *as Mr. Darc's Tales from Terror*, the story of the appearance in the graveyard became more of a fun anecdote, dismissed as probably some form of videotape noise and forgotten.

There were times when I sat there, alone in my area listening to the soundtrack of distant screams, that I felt something, an unease brought on by the "What if?" My mind would wander, and imagination combined with reality where I became aware that this haunt exuded an aura of malevolence that transcended mere mortal comprehension. It was spooky fun in the safe way that Halloween night is, watching scary movies or shows like *In Search Of...* and allowing yourself to feel the scare of the supernatural like Bigfoot, UFOs, demons, and vampires. You allow your imagination to create scenarios of things in the darkness of the night. But then, a group of guests would come through, and your energy and focus would become sinister, eliciting screams from them as you became their tormentor.

Then a short time later, I would experience something that could not be explained a glitch or reflection of light.

The night started easily enough. I would be working in the Morgue.

I picked up my costume, a pair of medical scrubs, and moved into the Dweller's dressing room. There, I would start my make-up process. I would talk with Alan and gain approval for what I wanted to do, and once he blessed the idea, adding his expertise, I set about adding the darkness of sunken eyes and grim features that would help tell the story of this mad morgue assistant who haunted the remnants of the medical facility. The Morgue was on the second floor and was a great scare. It was the last scare on that level, sending the guests down a stairwell and into a toxic chemical spill. It was proceeded by an intense set and scare based on the possession of a little girl. So, my station was between the sound of demonic voices, screaming possessed girls on one side, and the alarm klaxon of a chemical warning ion the other. Between those environments, my space was generally one of the best set experiences at Terror.

The guests would travel down a long hallway and into the set of a medical facility. A large sign hung above the opening with a simple word: Morgue. The smell of chemicals and rot was prevalent. The group turned a corner and emerged into a sickly green tiled room where hanging body forms in white bags hung from the ceiling. Each bag had dark red stains that gave the illusion of seeping rot from inside. The muffled sound of a heartbeat slowly thumped over the speakers.

The group would slowly move past the hanging medical bags as a light slowly started to strobe in an alternating pattern with the

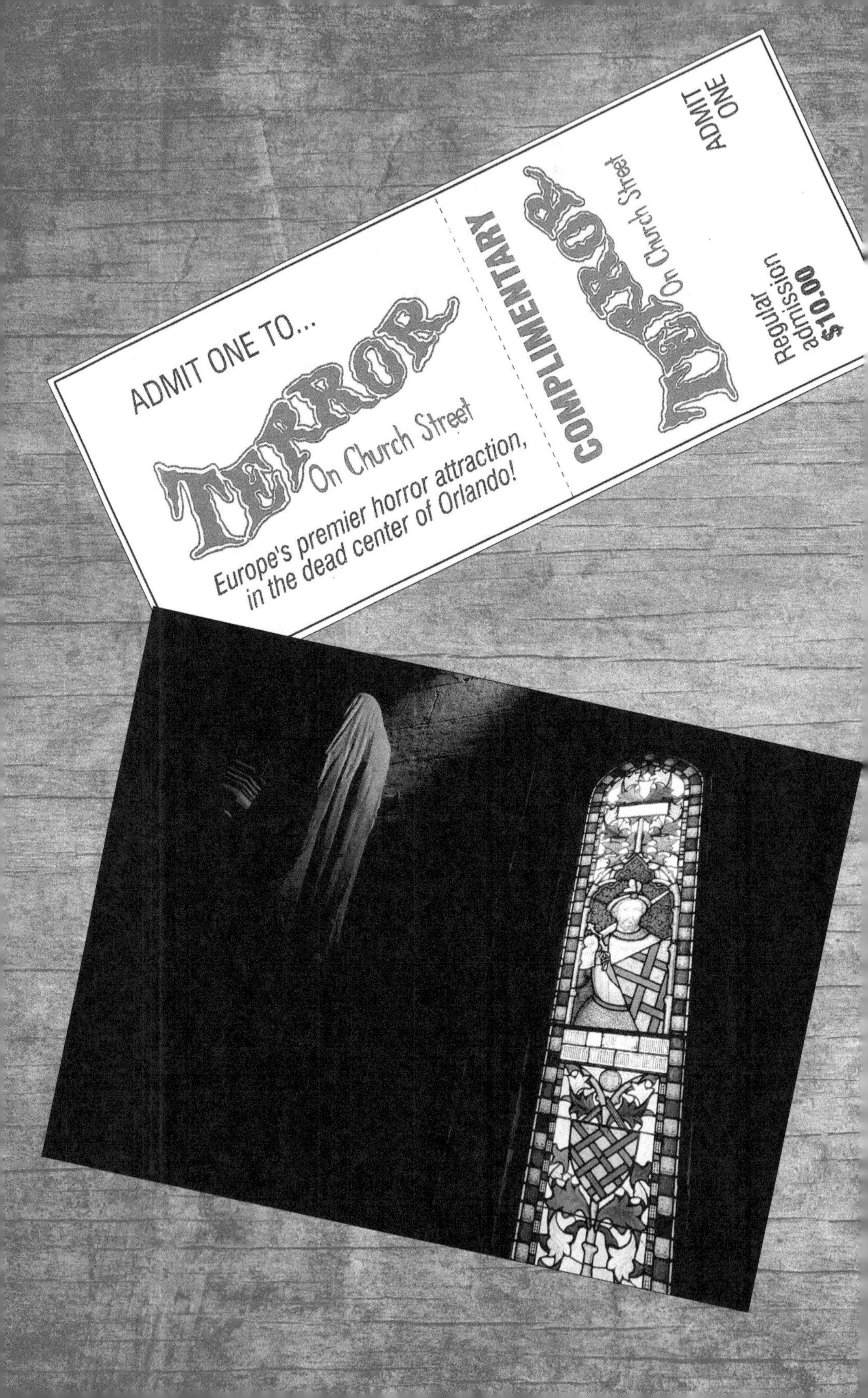

ADMIT ONE TO...
TERROR
On Church Street
Europe's premier horror attraction,
in the dead center of Orlando!

COMPLIMENTARY

TERROR
On Church Street

ADMIT ONE

Regular
admission
$10.00

heartbeat that created an unnerving effect. I watched the group from the corner through a small opening. I had a microphone and was able to taunt them as they tried to navigate the hanging bodies.

I would laugh, and then, slowly, in a truly deranged way, start to recite a twisted version of a children's nursery rhyme.

"Humpty Dumpty sat on a wall.

Humpty Dumpty had a great fall.

And all the king's horses and all the king's men…"

Then, reaching a crescendo, I would scream, "Couldn't put Humpty Dumpty together again!"

At that moment, I would usually trigger an effect in the room that connected all the bags together on an intricate trolley system and would start them to move back and forth around the room. As I started to reach for the button, I saw something in the room that lurched forward from the corner nearest my hiding spot and bound through the space. My first thought was it was another actor, playing a prank. The figure appeared dressed in white. The guests also saw it and screamed as it approached them. As they all ducked and weaved around the remnants of discarded bodies and the approaching figure, I paused. Who was that? With the moment of scare being robbed, I hit the button and the bodies started to move along their trolley path. I would move across my small room and then appear through an opening nearby for what was called an impact scare. As I leapt out, the group was looking behind them and turned to see me.

"Because I stole his brain!"

I pretended to bite into an ultra-realistic prop brain, supplied by Terror's resident make-up guru Alan Ostrander. I squeezed as I bit, and liquid splashed out at the group. A girl screamed and burst ahead of the group. Success! I lurched toward them, moving them from the room. The group started to run, exited, and disappeared, moving down a stairwell to the rest of the attraction. I turned to look back at the morgue set, expecting to see my prankster. There in the open doorway, I saw it.

It had the form of a man, but the clothing was fluid with no discernible edges of design, almost like a unitard. It looked at me. My eyes scanned up to lock eyes and connect, in that way humans do looking for some shared existence, but where the face should be was a blur. No features, no eyes, just a blur like an out of focus photo, a twisted apparition clad in ethereal white, its form shifting and writhing like a shadow. It's face, if it could be called such, was a blur of indistinct features, devoid of humanity yet brimming with malevolence. My brain felt alien in the experience of the new sensation. I didn't speak. I didn't move. I just stood there, waiting for something that would connect.

The faceless entity continued across the doorway and dissipated into a wall. The lock was gone. It was gone. I was overcome with a feeling of absolute dread. My stomach became queasy, and there was a thickness in the air of the room. I stood there for a few seconds, truly paralyzed as my brain tried to connect the dots. Another group was coming by that time, and I half-heartedly went through the bare minimum to move them through. I didn't feel well. I called down to the office and asked to be relieved. As I sat in the office, I explained what I saw and was met with two distinctly different reactions from different groups. One was disbelief, but the more prevalent one was "Oh, is that all?"

Later, I found out that there was an entity of some kind that was called Yellow Man. Many of the other performers had experience of some paranormal meeting. I wanted to know more, but there was no one cohesive reasoning behind the manifestations. The history behind his appearance ranged from the story that he had been a suicidal young man that hung himself in the Woolworth building to an entity that had been brought into the building from real tombstones that were used as props in the graveyard. I went home early that night and had a lot of trouble letting go of the experience.

I came back to Terror the next night and requested to work mostly as a "fisher" if possible. I couldn't shake the feeling of something otherworldly lurking in the shadows. I was able to spend a good amount of my time roaming the streets and helping generate excitement for the attraction. But there were also needs inside, and I would also be assigned a role within. At the same time, I was transitioning to a full-time role at Universal Studios Florida and worked less and less. Every time I came back, I always had a moment that something was aware that I was there, almost like the building was gleeful that I had returned, feeding off my moments of anxiety and dread. Then I was given a contract at Universal to play a dream role in the *Ghostbusters Spooktacular Live Show,* and I became devoted to that, alternating between chasing Class-five, full-torso, vaporous apparition as Ray, Peter, and Egon and shutting down the containment unit as Walter Peck.

After that, I only worked at Terror on Church Street a handful of times, and I always had the feeling that there was something there that was now watching me, knowing that I was one of the ones that saw it.

The last night I worked at Terror was during a big street party event: The Party To Die For! It was a sprawling downtown Orlando event that combined street festival fare, music, and acts with Terror on Church Street anchoring the event as a centerpiece. It was a busy night. There was a lot of excitement, and the energy was high.

That night, I played a Hannibal Lecter-inspired patient inside an iron jail cell. Guests would navigate around the three sides as I would taunt them through a leather face shield. At the perfect moment, I would grab the cell and pull off the heavy iron door and slam it to the side, stepping out into their space and coming face to cowering face with them. It was a truly fun role and very effective. As the night progressed, I felt more and more uneasy. The feeling of something watching me was prevalent. As one group came through, I did my bit.

"Tell me, have those lambs stopped their screaming?"

The guests stared at me in response to the odd question, moving around the hallway, protected by the safety of the cell bars. I tilted my head and then attacked, pulling the gate open and slamming it, creating a loud clang. I stepped into the hall, and they fled, screaming. I turned, entered the cell and returned the door to its spot, making sure it was secure. I turned and moved into the cell. I waited, listening for my cue. My back was to the hallway. I thought I heard someone enter the room and looked around. Was it time to break? Then, without any warning, the iron grate came unhinged and fell, catching me across the back of my skull. A sickening metal thud followed by the hollow feeling of pain. I almost passed out from the concussive hit.

I went to the hospital that night, having a slight concussion. Something had wanted to hurt me, and it was only going to get worse. I felt it, and I didn't want to go back.

That was my last night performing at Terror on Church Street. That incident combined with my good fortune of having another opportunity allowed me to move on.

As the next year progressed, I moved from performing at Universal into helping concept and design entertainment, including Halloween Horror Nights. My time at Terror absolutely prepared me for this, providing me with a solid foundation of haunted theatre, scare tactics, design, and immersive storytelling. David and team allowed me some great opportunities along with performing, including scripting, design, character creation, and media production. I would always brag about the experience and was always welcome to bring guests through the attraction. I went a handful of times, enjoying the dedication of that band of misfits. I will admit, there were some moments of dread as I turned certain corners or revisited the building, but they were overshadowed by melancholy. I missed the fun time I had and truly appreciated the opportunity that David Clevinger, Jack Neiberlein, and the rest of the Eternal Dwellers gave me. There are times that I still feel the excitement of being there. But I also know that something was there. I saw it, and more frighteningly, it saw me.

The last time I went into the building was the final auction. I walked through the space where many of the props and set pieces had been dismantled, but there was still something there. Soon after, the building was torn down and replaced. It is now a hotel. I hope whatever was there, whatever called that place home, was released to a different existence.

Terror on Church Street has been gone for decades, but anyone who experienced its darkened halls will testify that it stood as a beacon of terror, a rite of passage for thrill-seekers and horror aficionados alike. The legacy of fear it left behind endured, a testament to the power of imagination and the allure of the unknown.

Years later, as the building faced demolition, I revisited the site, hoping to find closure. Though the physical structure was no more, the lingering presence of the unknown lingered, a reminder of the mysteries that once inhabited those hallowed halls.

DARK FOREST
X-Sector
Park Entrance/Exit

IMAGE CREDITS

From the Haunters

Two Cherubs at Gravesite by J. Michael Roddy................II

Trap by J. Michael Roddy VII

Trick or ... by J. Michael Roddy VIII

Little Girl Lost by J. Michael Roddy XII

Through the Woods by J. Michael Roddy XV

Dianna Bennett..XVI
    Bruise from Bitemark by Dianna Bennett............................4

Michael Gavin 8
    Angel in Cemetery by Michael Gavin 8
    Top: Grave Silhouette in Fog by Michael Gavin 13
    Bottom Left: Baby Land 3 by Michael Gavin 13
    Bottom Right: Cherub Statue by Michael Gavin 13
    Top: Cemetery Road by Michael Gavin 14
    Middle: Foggy Cemetery by Michael Gavin 14
    "13" Sign by Michael Gavin................................14

Jeff Preston 18
    Skeleton Wall by Jeff Preston 18
    Skeleton with Rats by Jeff Preston.........................23
    Creepy Babydolls by Jeff Preston 26

Kevin Alvey 30
    Kevin and Krampus by Kevin Alvey 30
    Top: Horned Demon with Tusks by Kevin Alvey..............34
    Bottom: Lunging Monster by Kevin Alvey 34
    Top: Giant Eel Head by Kevin Alvey 39
    Bottom: Pumpkin Head Scarecrow by Kevin Alvey 39
    Hammerhead Box by Kevin Alvey 43

RANDY BATES **44**
    TOP: MAKEUP ART BY RANDY BATES. 47
    BOTTOM: RED GLOW BY RANDY BATES. 47
    BATES MOTEL HALLWAY BY RANDY BATES. 50
    TOP: UNDEAD COWBOY BY RANDY BATES. 54
    BOTTOM: UNDEAD SALOON GIRL BY RANDY BATES 54
    SCARY CLOWN BY RANDY BATES 61
    SCREAMING GIRL BY RANDY BATES. 61
    RESTLESS SOULS CEMETERY ENTRANCE BY RANDY BATES. 64
    UNDEAD BRIDE BY RANDY BATES. 67

GENE & JIM SCHOPF **68**
    FIELD OF SCREAMS ENTRANCE WITH THE GENE AND JIM BY GENE &
        JIM SCHOPF 68
    TOP: GENE SCHOPF BY GENE & JIM SCHOPF. 71
    BOTTOM: GENE SCHOPF AS JACK THE CLOWN BY GENE & JIM SCHOPF 71
    TOP: JIM SCHOPF BY GENE & JIM SCHOPF. 72
    BOTTOM: JIM SCHOPF AS THE GOBLIN MAYOR BY GENE & JIM SCHOPF 72
    JACK THE CLOWN BY GENE & JIM SCHOPF 76
    TOP: JACK CHASING GIRLS BY GENE & JIM SCHOPF. 80
    FOS EARLY DAYS SIGNAGE BY GENE & JIM SCHOPF 80
    BRANDING VICTIM BY GENE & JIM SCHOPF 85
    TOP: FOX 43 INTERVIEW BY GENE & JIM SCHOPF. 89
    BOTTOM: CUSTOM CHAINSAW BLADES BY GENE & JIM SCHOPF 89
    TOP: ASYLUM PATIENT BY GENE & JIM SCHOPF 92
    BOTTOM: TANNER SCHOPF AS BUTCHER PETE BY GENE & JIM SCHOPF. 92
    HAYRIDE BY GENE & JIM SCHOPF. 95
    NURSE ROOM BY GENE & JIM SCHOPF. 98
    WASTELANDERS BY GENE & JIM SCHOPF. 102

KYLE LAFLAMBOY **106**
    TOP: CREEPY DUO BY KYLE LAFLAMBOY 112
    BOTTOM: CREEPY CHILD BY KYLE LAFLAMBOY 112

SCOTT TATER LYND **120**
    TOP: SCOTT TATER LYND BY SCOTT TATER LYND. 120
    BOTTOM: GOBLIN MAKEUP BY SCOTT TATER LYND 120

RICKY BRIGANTE **128**
    #NOFILTER BY RICKY BRIGANTE 135

HALLOWEEN ENDS 2019 BY J. MICHAEL RODDY. **137**

DAVE COBB **138**
    TOP: AN EVENING WITH RAY BRADBURY BY DAVE COBB. 143
    BOTTOM: SIGNED LEAF AND BOOK BY DAVE COBB. 143
    MEETING RAY BRADBURY BY DAVE COBB 144

JESSICA DWYER. **148**

EDDIE MCLAURIN **158**
    TOP: EDDIE MCLAURIN 158
    BOTTOM: IN CHARACTER BY EDDIE MCLAURIN 158
    TOP: VAMPIRE BY EDDIE MCLAURIN 161
    MIDDLE: WOMAN SCREAMING BY EDDIE MCLAURIN 161

Bottom: Hurt Victims by Eddie McLaurin 161
Scary Clown in Neon by Eddie McLaurin 164
Bella and Eddie by Eddie McLaurin 167

Mike Schwalm **168**
Mike Schwalm and Child by Mike Schwalm 168
Top: Early Artwork Concepts by Mike Schwalm................171
Middle: Ride Concept Art by Mike Schwalm 171
Bottom: Current Fanart by Mike Schwalm 171
Top: Velociraptor by Mike Schwalm 175
Bottom: Childhood Mike Making Stuff by Mike Schwalm........175

Ed Terebus...**178**
Ed Terebus Being Attacked by Ed Terebus....................178
Erebus Signage by Ed Terebus...............................183
Masterminds of Erebus by Ed Terebus 183
Guinness World Recod Certificate by Ed Terebus.............184
Hearses Parked infront of Erebus by Ed Terebus.............187
Top: Early Version by Ed Terebus 188
Bottom: Current Version by Ed Terebus 188

Matthew Sanderson **192**

Christian Stokes **204**

J. Michael Roddy.......................................**216**
J. Michael Roddy with Living Dead by J. Michael Roddy......216
Cemetery Parking Sign by J. Michael Roddy 222
Terror on Church Street Vampire by J. Michael Roddy........228
Top: Terror on Church Street Ticket by J. Michael Roddy....232
Bottom: Hex - Alton Towers - Staffordshire by J. Michael Roddy ...232
Alton Towers - Staffordshirt by J. Michael Roddy 237
Lonely Ghost by J. Michael Roddy 238

**Discover more at
4HorsemenPublications.com**

10% off using HORSEMEN10